Retail
The Lifestyle
Banking

Retail
The Lifestyle Banking

Gautam Gan
Udayan Gan Chowdhury
Sreyashi Gan

ZORBA BOOKS

ZORBA BOOKS

Publishing Services by Zorba Books, November 2019

Website: www.zorbabooks.com
Email: info@zorbabooks.com

Cover designed by Hasnain

ISBN Print Book - 978-81-943110-6-5
ISBN eBook - 978-81-943110-7-2

Zorba Books Pvt. Ltd. (opc)
Sushant Arcade,
Next to Courtyard Marriot,
Sushant Lok 1, Gurgaon – 122009, India

INSPIRATION
Ratnabali Gan

DEDICATED TO :

Mr. Ujwal Thakar
Pioneer in Retail Banking in India.

Mr. Gautam Vir
Revered international banker, popularly known as "Turn Around Man".

Contents

Foreword

Banking in India has been walking the Retail way since CITI and Standard Chartered bank made their foray into Retail banking in this country way back in 1986. Prior to this, Retail banking was in existence in General Banking form. The advent of the above two banks in the Retail arena with initial Retail products and distributed risk in the market, marked the renaissance in Banking industry in the Indian sub-continent. *Spicer and Oppenheim,* the UK based renowned consultant group had expressed in 1987 that as far as Retail Banking is concerned in India, "Sky is the limit." Since then, this mega retail market in India has been witnessing an accelerated growth year to year and entry of a long line of competition with array of products, strategies and human skills.

Standing close to the second decade of the 20th century, we see Retail banking in a new avatar where day to day banking transactions and guiding laws/ practices have taken a back seat and the main focus has shifted to Strategies, Channel management, innovative Products, Service quality, Handling competition, Human Resource, etc. In fact, Retail Banking is the most exciting subject in Banking science at present dealing with and driven by the behavioural pattern of people, community by community, segment by segment. Its cornerstone is human psychology. There are indeed multiple of books in the market on day to day banking operations and procedures. However, there is an insignificant attempt to unfold a threadbare discussion on how mature is Retail Banking now after almost four decades of its growth in India. What actually is or should Retail Banking be or is expected from it. Hardly do we find an effort to study Retail Banking in the light of Human Psychology.

This book thus is rightly termed *"Retail – The Lifestyle Banking,"* which is a sincere effort to explore not only the spirit of this business vertical in banking in India but also to assess how human life and Retail banking are married together with a touch of time. At the end of it, Retail banking revolves around the expectations of individuals and the delivery of the expectations. Additionally, since Retail Banking is about the desires and expectations of banking population, the business is handled by a huge population in the retail banking arena. Hence, this has become a part of the life of Retail Bankers across the country irrespective of their ranks and responsibilities. The book has thus also touched the Human Resource field in Retail Banking and has accessed the personal likes, dislikes, aspirations and heartbreaking stories of people who are the key factors in running and developing Retail Banking in India. Retail is people's banking and it's driven by people hence psychology of both the groups cannot be ignored.

Our book does not essentially deal with the grammar of Banking, its rules, and regulations. The book "Retail – The Lifestyle Banking" is narrated in a storytelling mode where it talks of a new vertical of business which was born only three decades back and showed a quick growth along with the growth of IT sector which also has a similar vintage in this soil. It's a story of a business vertical in Banking industry which enjoyed tremendous support from IT sector and with the change in people's Life Style, grew both physically and spiritually. We shall be happy if it is happy reading for the readers and also users in Retail Banking world in India.

Preface from the
Co-author – Udayan Gan Chowdhury

Not every day does a son get to pen lines for his father's book. But the very thought of being a co-author to someone from whom you would have learnt the ABCs of Retail Banking is quite unnerving.

Some lessons are imparted without a focused intent and absorbed by the subconscious. I remember those discussions over the dining table between my father Mr. Gautam Gan and my grandfather Mr. Bikram Kumar Gan who was also a retired banker of the then Grindlays Banks (now part of Standard Chartered Bank). The discussions ranged from banking processes to office politics, from RBI regulations to tricky customers, from inspiring bosses to the committed team, the common theme being Retail Banking. It was two generations sharing the challenges of today and the learning from yesterday, the most enlightening conversation that a school-going child like myself could get exposure to. I absorbed them not as a domain but as a way of life of a Retail Banker.

Naturally I was more conversant about banking processes, payment instruments etc. than what could be expected at my age. When I was doing my MBA, the classroom lectures and bolded lines from fat curriculum books reverberated those concepts I had absorbed over dinner. It was almost like an unintentional run-ahead preparation that my father and grand-father took me through, empowering me to easily relate and appreciate what was now my subject of specialization.

As if it was all scripted, the campus recruitment landed me in the Banking domain capability of my first organization and though I had aspired to follow the path of a branch banker, I was placed in this sweet spot between IT and Business that is called "Business Analysis." It gave me the opportunity to know about banking practices from clients around the world and the ability to apply technology to improve them. After more than a decade of working with three global IT consulting companies and majorly with Banking clients, I still hold dear the memories of my dining table discussions. To this day, when confronted with a challenging problem to solve, the anecdotes from my father and grandfather take me to the basics and help me propose innovative alternatives.

I feel obliged today to be able to contribute to this book and dedicate this piece of work to the two gentlemen who laid down my foundations and made me capable to pen a few lines for you. Thank you Baba and Dadan.

RETAIL BANKING

CUSTOMER IN BRANCH....

THE NEXT DECADE

Retail Banking is quite an ocean in itself and to write about its future in the scope of this book would be to undermine the depth of the domain or my respect of it.

Therefore, I chose to talk about a micro-domain in retail banking that we all have interfaced with – it is called Branch Banking, and a part of it that pertains to the customer's experience in a branch for a typical transaction. In the era of electronic channels like ATM, Internet Banking, Phone Banking, Mobile apps and wearables (Smart Watch) the usefulness of Branches are being questioned. I call this a very myopic and transactional mind-set. Machines can add efficiency to our lives by performing repetitive tasks with accuracy and consistency. What we call Artificial Intelligence continues to be a set of complex rule-based behaviours programmed by a human. The possibility of services from a machine continues to be constrained by the extent of human imagination on the range of problems or interactions in an ecosystem. Besides the emotional connect is something machines are not going to replace in the foreseeable future, precisely why it is called 'human touch'. Till that happens we can expect an era of harmonious 'co-existence' of human and machine complementing each other to elevate the levels of quality, efficiency and convenience in branch banking services.

Most of you would agree that the science of deduction is much more dependable than Crystal Gazing. So, let us try to deduce the future of Branch Banking by looking into the needs of the industry and the technology trend of our times.

The underlying principle of application of technology is that it is driven by Business Outcomes. While science is a pursuit of the possible not necessarily with a goal, technology is funded by Business and lives to serve it. Any technological application therefore, for it to be a success, be accepted widely and sustain through an appreciable length of time, must serve a larger business goal. And to put it in its crudest form, a business goal can be broadly of 2 types: A. to earn more money or B. to slow down losing money.

Let us see some examples to illustrate:

IMMEDIATE GOAL OF A PROJECT	LEADS TO LARGER GOAL	ULTIMATE GOAL	
		EARN MORE MONEY	SLOW DOWN LOSING MONEY
Improve the Usability or Availability	1. Customer Retention 2. Customer Acquisition	More Customers, More Revenue	
Reduce Turn Around Time / Increase Efficiency of a process	1. Need for less work force 2. Increased convenience to customers leading to Customer Acquisition	More Customers, More Revenue	Less spend on salaries
Increase Accuracy of a process	1. Less chances of rework 2. Lower Operational risk		1. Less spend on salaries for human effort on rework 2. Less chances of Regulatory fine or Cancelling License
Improve Reporting to Management or Regulator	1. Tighten process controls 2. Unavoidable regulatory need		1. Stop revenue leakages 2. Less chances of Regulatory fine or Cancelling License

With that in mind, let us look into the evolution of technology in banks over the past few decades and what market needs it has tried to address. That coupled with the needs of today should give us a fair guess into what's likely to come up.

Payments are one of the corner-stones of banking and together with withdrawals and deposits, has been one of the key services traditionally provided over the counter by branches through ages. Clearly payments in the open market which was predominantly cash-based till a few decades ago, has been replaced largely by the plastic card.

Introduction of Plastic Money: The first cards were introduced as a way for the merchant to capture the clients signature on an ink-imprint of the embossed image on a paper. Soon enough the introduction of magnetic tape on plastic card enabled it to store key payment information. With the emergence of the card schemes or payment networks like Visa, Mastercard etc. this technology was harnessed to exchange payment information over global secured networks and perform settlements in real-time.

Rise of Alternate Channels: Cards started getting used in ATMs for withdrawal from one's own account or at merchant's EFTPOS terminals for secure payment across banks. This was a notch up in convenience and banks were happy to invest in scaling up their infrastructure to spread ATMs and EFTPOS terminals because of the massive return on investment in the form of reduced staffing at the counters as queues as customers take to these alternate channels of payments and transaction.

Promoting Self-service: With Gen X and Gen Y showing their savvy to electronic gadgets, banks found a way to kill two birds in a single hit. They called it 'Self-service'. While the concept appeals to customers as an empowerment allowing them to take control of their own accounts, it passes on the effort of the banking staff in smaller nitty-gritty's of daily banking because now the customer will do it themselves. Banks invested on their internet banking platforms to include services like changing PINs of Cards, Applying for an Account, downloading Statements, Checking Balances and such activities which would occupy the bandwidth of branch staff for unproductive needs (something that will not get them any revenue). To provide further support banks setup their call centres providing nearly round the clock support. Integrated Voice Recognition (IVR) integrated with telephony performed a seamless routing of customer calls to appropriate departments with sufficient needs analysis and contextual input for the executives to action on. For standard requests like password reset, requesting a duplicate card or making a card payment, telephone banking was equipped with enough intelligence to handle the transaction end to end without human intervention.

Security and Convenience: If one has to summarize and name the theme of the advancements in payment space over the past decade, it would surely be called 'Security and Convenience.' This is when we saw technology take quick bends at inflection points that soon rendered the previous versions obsolete. For example, the magnetic chip technology replaced the so-far trusted magnetic tape for the increased security and anti-theft measures it provided. Thus the 'please swipe the card' notification at the EFTPOS / ATM' was replaced by 'please insert the card.' As fraudsters got smarter, banks introduced the concept of 2 factor authentication which involved A. something you have (e.g. Card) and B. something you know (e.g. secret PIN). With the advent and popularity of smartphones, adapters were manufactured that could be plugged into a smart phone and can enable the swiping and inserting of the card. The phone's keypad could then be used for entering the pin and its network could be used to transmit the payment data securely over an app. This was an economic way for small traders to provide the facility of card payment without buying an EFTPOS terminal.

Touchless and Cardless: Next came the age of Near-Field Communication (NFC). The technology would allow a magnetic card to transmit data to a payment terminal without physical contact, but only with a close proximity for a few seconds. As smart phones became smarter, payment applications (apps) evolved to digitize the plastic card. A mobile wallet, as it came to be known can now hold the information of multiple cards. As a step further towards security and convenience, PINs got replaced by bio-metric signatures like fingerprint and iris-scan. The customer and the phone therefore becomes one single entity. As long as one has a phone with adequate battery to communicate over NFC, one can make payments and withdraw money from ATMs.

Identity Simplification:

Too long had people required to remember their IDs and passwords. With passwords getting simplified to bio-metrics, it was time to eliminate the need to remember user IDs. A single customer ID had already unified the entire relationship portfolio of a customer under one banner covering all products and services they were engaged with and provide a "single customer view." Now it was turn to move to something less taxing to commit to memory than a 9 or 10 digit customer ID. In the past five years or so banks have started extending the facility to link social unique IDs to accounts. E.g. Email ID or Phone Number. A customer can therefore just share their bank name and phone number with a party who owes money to him/her. The payer can trigger a transaction from his bank with the Phone Number. When the transaction hits the receiver's bank, the phone number is used to retrieve the mapped account number to which the amount is credited. Similarly, one can pay to someone's mobile and allow them to collect the amount at an ATM. In this case the bank shares a one-time unique code with the recipient which needs to be keyed into the ATM console to identity oneself and collect the amount.

Hope this crash course of trending banking tech has served its purpose of showing you how rapidly Banking has been evolving with the help of technology. I reserve the latest and the best for our final prediction of the future.

THE NICE CUSTOMER

Let us now turn our attention to business demand. Branches have been since the birth of banking, the point of interaction between the customers and the bank staff. Advent of electronic channels has largely reduced the flow of traffic into branches, but there are still banking needs that need to be fulfilled with manual intervention in a face to face interaction. This brings me back to my dining table conversations and lessons learnt. I remember my father quoting the instance of a "Nice Customer" which describes an apparently insignificant random walk-in that is ignored by banks / restaurants / post-office and such customer service industries, and how it can impact their business. As I indulge in the fond recollection of such a treasured lesson, let me allow myself the liberty to tweak it a bit to suit specifically the banking context. In my version this is how it looks:

I am a nice customer. I'm the one who never complains,
no matter what kind of service I get.

I go into a Bank and wait quietly. I see you treat me like everyone else,
when I have been keeping my money with you since ages.

I am patient while you try to talk me into your products being
completely oblivious of what I need or like.

Sometimes someone that came after I did gets attended to before me,
but I don't complain, I just wait.

I never nag. I never criticize. I never make a scene.
I'm the nice customer.

And…

I'm the customer who never comes back!

A customer who never comes back costs an organization revenue, repute as well as potential business from other customers by word of mouth.

So, what does a nice customer want from a branch experience? Below is what most of you will agree:

- To be identified without introducing himself
- Not to be kept waiting in a long queue
- To be kept informed on his requests without following up and be prompt at resolving them
- Have a connected experience consistently across channels, physical or digital
- Be engaged in contextual conversations rather than random marketing attempts

The experience of a typical retail banking customer can be summarized as below:

- A customer or prospect walks into a branch and waits in a queue, to draw a token from a kiosk where he selects the type of service he is after
- In more "customer-centric" branches, there is a dedicated lobby manager who greets the customer, usually with a fancy iPad, but does the exact same job as a kiosk
- There is no expectation setting with the customer at a branch. One has no idea how long it is likely to take before his turn comes and can only make and intelligent guess by the turn around time of the queue as "will take long" or "shouldn't take long," the word 'long' being the highly subjective quantification of time
- During the time of wait, the bank expects the customer/ prospect to be curious about the products and services and pick up one of the brochures stacked somewhere in the branch. The customer however finds it more fulfilling to immerse himself in social media on his phone.

- When his turn comes, he must explain the context of his visit. Sometimes, one visits the branch after his endless attempts with the phone banking has yielded no result. The branch behaves as a completely dissociated channel and adds to the customer's frustration by asking him to narrate the background all over again.

- If he has to open an account, it takes days for him to be operational with the logistical roadblocks of Background Verification and delivery of ATM/Debit Card & PIN to reach his postal address followed by a process of activation to follow.

- There is no follow up on his service requests from the bank's end. He needs to call the phone banking or visit the branch again to make an enquiry on the status.

Therefore, there is a disappointingly and frustratingly wide gap between the expectations and the experience. Now let us find out how the power of technology of our times can help a bank live up to the expectations of a Nice Customer and help them continue as a loyal and happy client.

FUTURE OF CUSTOMER EXPERIENCE IN A BRANCH

Appointment Booking: They say "Time is Money". And in this age of information and connectivity, people grow restless at the thought of uncertainty. In a world where there is mutual respect for each other's time, the practice of casually walking in to check availability, is going out of vogue. From medical centres to restaurants, people prefer to make an appointment and "block their calendars". Seems only befitting that for a transaction at a bank, a customer is able to book a time slot before visiting the branch.

To achieve this, internet banking platforms, accessible using web browsers or mobile apps should be integrated to the staff calendars at branches and be able to find the availability of staff by skill (service offered) and location of the branch. A more tech-savvy way would be to use voice commands over Intelligent Voice Assistant like Google, Alexa, Cortana or Siri. Let us see an example of such a conversation.

The customer is on his couch in the living room and speaks to Google Home Assistant.

Customer: "Okay Google, please book me an appointment at the nearest HDFC bank branch tomorrow"

Google: "Sure. What service would you like to go for?"

Customer: "I would like to get a Demand Draft"

Google: "And what time would you prefer"

Customer: "Around mid-day"

Meanwhile Google checks the nearest branch of the mentioned bank and the calendar of staff with the required skill-set

Google: "I can book you an appointment between 2pm and 2.30pm tomorrow at the Gariahat Branch of HDFC Bank for getting a Demand Draft. Do you want me to book it?"

Customer: "Yes please"

Google: "Your appointment is now booked. I will block your personal calendar on Google as well to give you a reminder before 2 hours"

2 hours before the appointment, the customer is dining at a restaurant. Google assistant springs to life on his smart watch and speaks out: "This is to remind you about your appointment at 2pm in Gariahat Branch of HDFC Bank. Let me know if you want me to reschedule it". Customer acknowledges the reminder on the smart watch.

In Branch Customer Experience: I remember the 90s when the then new generation banks spawned in Indian market. This new breed comprising HDFC Bank, ICICI Bank, IDBI Bank and AXIS Bank brought in a fresh air of customer service with their best in class infrastructure and energetic customer service team at the branches. However, I always wondered why my grandfather would continue to visit the same bank that he had been banking with all through his life and particularly one specific branch of it. The apparent reason was its proximity to our home, but something told me that even if we had moved to another home, my grandpa would still hold his loyalty to that branch. One visit with him to the branch made it obvious – it is the recognition. Human beings seek recognition. By recognition here I do not mean appreciation (which is used in most corporate contexts). It is the feel-good when you are identified among a crowd just by your face; it is the connection you feel when people remember you, your situation, your need, the last conversation with you. This connection, in those days grew to the extent that customers insisted to be serviced by one specific individual and he/she knew personal things like the customer's family, where his son works, which school his grandchild goes to, the state of his health etc.

By what my childhood brain could infer, this connection was spontaneous and not intentional, agenda-based to get more sales on the books, as it is these days. In those times, there was less drive from management to treat customers as leads for future opportunities and to count your time with the customer and measure the return on this investment. The result was a natural relationship-building leading to relationship-backed need-based selling and most importantly a very loyal customer base.

Times have changed now. Banks and all other Customer Service industries believe in treating customers as just another "token" and the special long term connection between a customer and a banker is replaced by the philosophy of "being agnostic" and providing a standardized uniform service to every customer. This factory model of treating customers as products in an assembly line and treating them the same way as the other one, does not work. A people-industry with real emotions requires human-centric approach; and if you treat customers like products, customers will treat you back that way and hop from one brand to another just with the motivation of a few Basis Points of Interest or by throwing cheap freebies like one-time fee-waivers. These apparently insignificant differentiators become determining factors when customers do not have a relationship to value. Banks around the globe have now acknowledged that the cost of acquiring a new customer is 5 times that of retaining an existing customer, when you factor in the cost of advertising, processing, issuing customer onboarding materials like plastic cards, welcome letters etc. Further, increasing customer retention by 5% can increase profits from 25-95% and the success rate of selling to a customer you already have is 60-70%, while the success rate of selling to a new customer is 5-20%. Customer retention is therefore a key priority for banks.

So let us see if the technology of our times can give us the power to strike a balance between providing personalized treatment to customers and delivering staff-independent standardised services.

Customer Identification/Recognition: Application of Bio-metrics has come a long way, from finger print recognition to iris scanning to face recognition. Not just to unlock smartphones, biometrics are being used in a number of industries to identify customers. Some of you would have seen cameras at the Immigration counters in airports. The image captured by these are run against a database of persons of interest from national and international stakeholders e.g. Interpol and flagged to the Immigration officer if there is a match with a reasonable confidence. Thus Biometrics, driven by Artificial Intelligence can play a strong role in Customer Identification. Using this principle branches can install cameras around doorways in different angles to captures profiles of incoming customers. To enhance the accuracy of identification, walk-ways leading from the entrance to the inside of a branch could be designed in a way that makes a person turn left and right so that the image is captured from all angles. These different images can be stitched together to build a 3D model that makes it easier to compare with the photo of the customer on the records. With an adaptive self-learning Artificial Intelligence running at the background, the accuracy of the matches increase progressively each time the customer steps into the branch. Banks may also choose to reserve the investment on the physical re-design of the branch (cameras, walk-way etc.) for more 'Premium' branches and go for economic alternatives of identification such as enabling NFC (Near Field Communication) detectors at the welcome kiosk where the customer can simply touch his/her Debit/Credit card with the bank or mobile phone with a smart wallet (e.g. Google/Apple Pay) which has the Debit/Credit card information configured. Obviously this alternative requires an active effort on the customer's end to identify oneself but is seamlessly integrated into the usual workflow of walking up to the kiosk.

Welcome Message: Once identified, it is important to deliver that "feel-good" to the customer by informing them that "we recognized you" and what could be a better way to do that, than a Welcome Message. Premium branches that have a lobby manager to meet and greet will get the information about the walk-in customer on a Branch Tablet with a full 360 degree view of the customer. That will cover the portfolio of accounts with the bank, open service requests and complaints (if any), last few interactions with different banking channels (Phone-banking, Internet Banking, Branch etc.). In addition to these notes around any shop talk captured during these interactions (e.g. customer had a plan to go for a Euro trip) will be shown as a tip to lead the conversation. In addition, if the customer has shared his social network IDs in the banking portal sometime and given a consent to access his social profile, then the 360 degree profile view will also show things like his Birthday or Anniversary date etc. Imagine how this revolutionizes the experience of a customer:

Present Day:

"Hello Sir, how can we help you today? Can you tell us your Name or Account Number pl?

The Future:

"Good Morning Mr. Sharma. Nice to see you again. Happy to inform you that the request to top-up your credit limit that you submitted in the Worli branch last week has been approved and the new limit has been applied to your card. Is it that or something else that brings you here today?

……By the way, you were planning for a Euro-trip. Is it an anniversary special holiday Sir; I think its coming up by the 15th of this month, isn't it? Would you like us to arrange Travel-money or a Forex Card for the trip?"

Isn't it spectacular, how the power of getting the right information and staying connected to the pulse of the customer can change the levels of customer experience delivery?

The above scenario would be more applicable to an HNI (High Net-worth Individual) or Affluent segment focused branch in a premium locale. For branches that focus more on retail segments, the branch could be too crowded for a Lobby Manager to strike a quality conversation with a client. To tailor the solution, the channel of communication should be picked according to the target segment. In this case, the welcome message could be sent to the customer's mobile phone leading to an interactive need-analysis. The welcome message will serve to address the customer by his name, adding the personal touch and make an intelligent guess about the type of service that he is here for today, based on his past interactions, open service requests etc. like in our example the request to top-up credit card limit. The interactive menu on the smart phone will be driven by a chatbot integrated to Artificial Intelligence that operates on the bank's CRM (Customer Relationship Management) tool. Thus the chatbot will give the customer the experience of chatting with a human being at the back office who knows about the customer's profile, open requests etc. and can also navigate the customer to other services or products that he is interested in. Should the customer seek for something the chatbot is yet to learn about (in its adaptive learning curve), the chatbot will route the chat to a human user at the call centre who can attend to exceptional cases.

Let us now rewind and travel 30 years back, to witness the emergence of retail banking and how has the lifestyle of Indian population gradually went through a transformation.

RETAIL BANKING – DEFINITION

"What is Retail Banking?" - This has baffled many a banker and often they are found to evade the question with a smiling reply "If not asked, I know but if you ask me, I know not". The reason being, various banks have segregated their Retail business from Whole Sale ones on different parameters. However, to end the controversy, people across banking industry seem to come to a compromise that Retail Banking essentially deals with House Hold Individuals.

On the basis of the above understanding of Retail business, banks have designed their Retail segmentation as below:

Purely individuals where Deposit, Loan or any other relationship are solely in the name/s of individual persons – like Sharad Srivastav, Anil Kumar, Kalpana Joshi e.t.c. These individuals may operate any account in their sole or joint names even in the form of business accounts in proprietorship, partnership or Private Limited companies.

But when it comes to Limited companies or Corporate Business, it goes to the domain of Whole Sale or Corporate Banking business.

In addition to the above, Non-profit bodies like Trusts, Clubs, Associations, NGO e.t.c fall under the purview of Retail Banking.

To clarify further, accounts of Banks and big Financial entities do fall under the jurisdiction of Treasury.

For a long time after the advent of Retail Banking as an independent business in India, Business verticals or Profit Centres were involved in fighting with each other over ownership of Business in reference to Retail Business. However, it's good that the apple of discord no more exists and Business is as it is with Retail segments of the banks.

Scope of Retail Banking in India

The general expectation while describing the scope of Retail Banking in the country is the writer should fill pages with statistics supporting his statements. But we shall take a different route – by recapitulation of a night at a party.

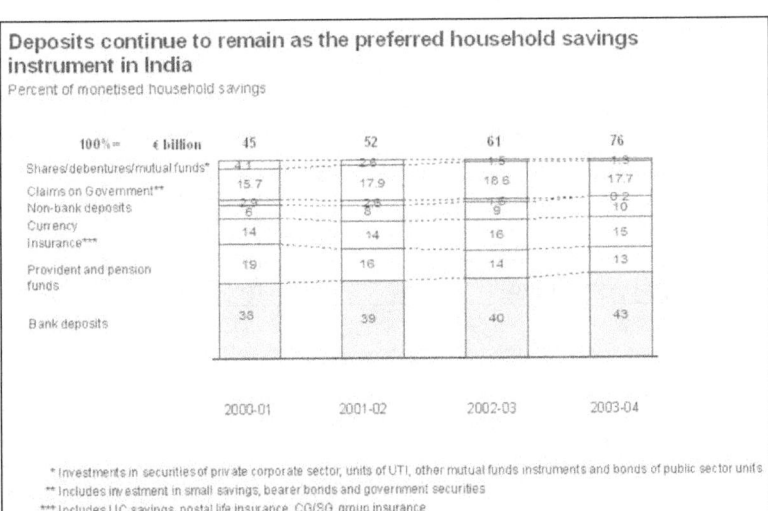

Deposits continue to remain as the preferred household savings instrument in India

Percent of monetised household savings

100% = ₹ billion	45	52	61	76
Shares/debentures/mutual funds*	4.1	2.8	1.5	1.3
Claims on Government**	15.7	17.9	18.6	17.7
Non-bank deposits	7.2	7.8	9	0.2 / 10
Currency Insurance***	14	14	16	15
Provident and pension funds	19	16	14	13
Bank deposits	38	39	40	43
	2000-01	2001-02	2002-03	2003-04

* Investments in securities of private corporate sector, units of UTI, other mutual funds instruments and bonds of public sector units
** Includes investment in small savings, bearer bonds and government securities
*** Includes LIC savings, postal life insurance, CG/SG group insurance
Source: RBI, McKinsey analysis

In 1988 when Standard Chartered Bank had decided to make foray into Retail Market in India, they engaged M/s Spicer & Oppenheim, the renowned consultant firm of UK to examine the scope of Retail Banking market in India. They had camped in India for quite some time and often used to call Retail Banking officers like us from all the major cities in the country for meetings. Ujwal Thacker took the lead from India platform and was in close touch with Spicers. There was a party thrown on the last day by the India management of StanC where I had asked one of them on their finding about the scope of Retail Banking business in India. I still remember the single sentence response– "As regards scope of Retail Banking in this country, Sky is the Limit". This explains all, I believe. Statistical figures will change every year with growth of population, their socio economic status, segment behaviour, purchase power etc. but the overall scope in the market with 125 crores of people will not change. The following MIS, although a bit old, may give a glimpse of size of the market before we travel to more important areas.

Six Distinct Income Segment in India		
Income Segment	Annual House Hold Income. (Rs. in '000)	Estimated Size - Mio
HNI	> 5000	0.06
Affluent	1000 – 5000	2.9
Lower Affluent	500 – 1000	9
Mass Affluent	200 – 500	48
Mass Individuals	90 – 200	70
Lower Income	< 90	66

~65% of household income is concentrated in the mass affluent and affluent segments

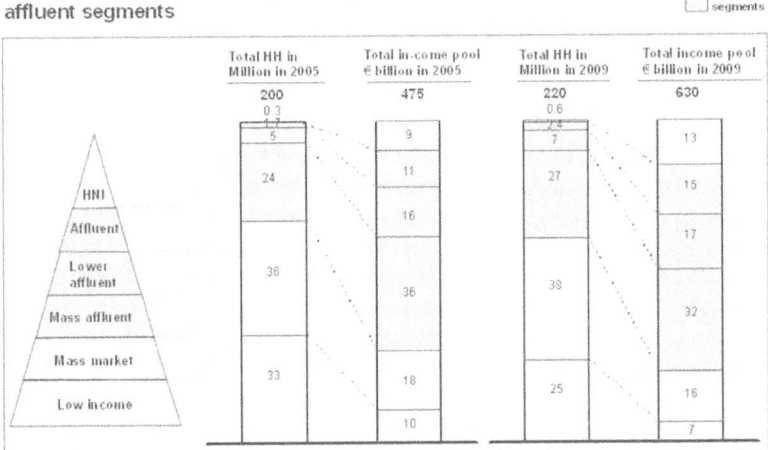

The target segments and deposit pools are concentrated in the top 8 cities

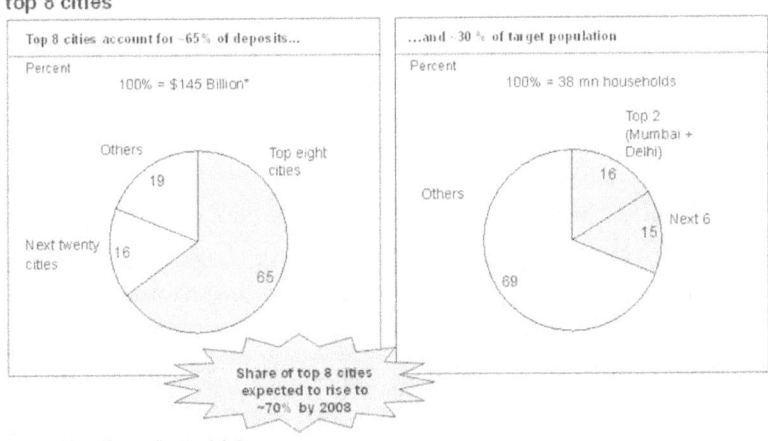

* Based on the top 100 deposit centers in India

RETAIL BANKING - EVOLUTION & REVOLUTION

Let us take a quick look at how Retail Banking rolled through evolution and revolution and finally is dancing in the ring in its present Avatar. Retail Banking very much existed, dissolved in the main stream banking in the form of General Banking and in the form of traditional products like normal Savings, Current, Term Deposits, Recurring Deposits etc. Record prompts that in the initial stage, in

Standard Chartered Bank (The then Chartered Bank) there was no Savings account. For individuals, only personal current accounts were entertained. The banks, in general, had a pyramid structure where on one side deposits used to be mobilised from all sources and the same was to be invested in the forms of Loans & Advances, Overdraft etc primarily to Corporates, mid-Corporates, SME sectors. Credit to Individuals was not in focus as part of business strategy and personal loans were allowed under consideration on case to case basis. So far it was an easy going banking till late 70s.

But Time is ruthless and in its kingdom nothing is permanent or stable. By early eighties Bankers began to think differently when mainly the Foreign Banks, started relooking at their business style due to increasing competition in Wholesale market and pressure on bottom line as a natural consequence. There were other factors too. It was the growing awareness of Risk in Wholesale banking business. It was identified that the risk associated with Wholesale business was concentrated against the distributed risk in Retail business. Let us take an example:

Suppose an amount of Rs.300 Crores was lent to a company in Corporate sector. While everything was going well, if suddenly on a bad morning there is reversal of fortune with the same borrower, the whole of 300 crores will be washed in one go and the same amount along with huge interest accrued will be provided by the bank and eventually written off from the balance sheet.

But if the same amount is given as Personal Loans to three lacs Individuals, the exposure per person will be Rs.1,00,000/- only. Now, it is next to impossible that these three lacs individual borrowers will immediately become defaulters.

Similarly is the case of Deposits. When a Corporate customer places 100 Crores of deposit, they usually keep it for short time pending next investment in business. In such cases, Banks find it difficult to plan investment of the fund because of volatility and uncertainty involved in such bulk deposits. But if the same amount of 100 crores are mobilised from one lac individuals, all these customers cannot knock the door of the banks for immediate withdrawal unless, of course, there is a Run in the bank for whatever may be the reason. This is the ground reality as far as the difference between Wholesale and Retail Banking business. *It's the concentrated risk against distributed risk which banks started realizing.*

Additionally, the higher spread of profit in Retail Banking seemed more lucrative than in Wholesale Banking where the growing competition in limited market was leading to back to back offers by competition thus to shrinking interest and fee income against threat of risk of bulk exposure.

1970s onward, there was a slow change in socio economic soil of the land as purchase power of individuals marked a steady increase and the last two decades of the bygone century witnessed people getting uplifted from level to level thus giving boost to Consumerism. On one hand, consumer durables started flooding the markets with growing desire of people to possess, and on the other, their income levels showed a positive graph which opened doors for Equate Monthly Schemes (EMI). How? let us look at an example as under :

In mid 70s, we witnessed massive entry of Television in the market. Let us peep through the window of Mr. Amit Misra, a State Govt employee with wife and two children, who was happily running his household with no demand from wife or children. One day, the next door neighbour, Biman Babu, brought a black and white TV home. Same evening, when Amit Babu returned home dragging his tired self he found no one. Maid informed that his family members are next door watching TV. Amit went for rest. His wife returned with kids and all of them were with broad smile describing how enchanting was the TV show. Amit concentrated in his news paper which he cannot read in the morning due to morning rush for office. This continued for a week or so. One day Amit Babu came home to a long faced wife and silent children. Up on asking, they narrated about the bad experience they had that evening in Biman Babu's house. Biman Babu's wife candidly pointed her displeasure on this every day routine of Amit's wife's visiting their house with kids to watch TV programmes. Now, what was the repercussion on Amit Babu? He might have been upset about his inability to afford a TV for his family. The price of a TV around that time was around Rs,10,000/- which, for Amit, was a huge expense with his meagre earning. Imagine, if at this juncture if a bank offers him a consumer durable loan repayable in three years against an EMI of Rs.350/-. How this can psychologically affect Amit ? He would jump for the TV since a monthly spend of Rs.350/- will be affordable to him. He will hardly think or calculate that the offered EMI plus processing fee carry a hidden interest rate as high as 22%.

This psychological impact on salaried individuals or individuals in other professions brought in Consumerism in a quick pace. The market across the country saw the flood of luxury goods ushering in living comforts. Starting from Televisions, Refrigerators, Washing Machines, Air Conditioners and so on came with array of models, features and benefits within the reach of common people to whom these were hitherto unaffordable. And, to banks and financial institutions this new business opened doors for higher profit as against the squeezed spread in Wholesale deals with Corporates and mid-Corporates that too with a comfort of lower and distributed Risks. Again, this evolution in Consumerism paved way for penetration into mass market for the Banks and gradually the inclusiveness was deep and wide with a continuous process of "Push & Pull".

In the Corporate world, it was the story of connection and contacts. Such business deals happened in social meets, parties, clubs, tennis lawns and golf turf.

Mr. Rodger Wright of Standard Chartered while wiping his face with towel after some rounds of Golf meets Mr. Dhanuka of

Dhan Cement over beer when they settle a deal of, say 50 Crores of Over Draft limit at an interest rate of X%. Matter used to end there and after due completion of securing documentations, business was on. But the age we are discussing i.e. end 1980s, potrays a changed scenario. Here the bank officials are entrants from Management schools or from other banks with relevant experiences unlike their predecessors who had only strong family background. These Corporate Bankers of new generation knew the language of Business only. In the new age, the deal settled by Mr. Right was no more a guaranteed one. After few days Mr. Suranjan Bose of Amex might meet Dhanuka offering a lower rate of interest with few other facilities and snatched the business of Dhan Cement from Standard Chartered. The Dhanukas in the Borrowers' world started taking full advantage of this poaching game and through offers and counter offers the interest rates were under pressure directly affecting the profitability. This is when Banks started turning their attention to Retail Banking for higher spread and lower risks.

Much before this change was advancing slowly, the financial market got filled with all types of competitors as under:

- Foreign Banks
- Nationalized Banks
- Old Private Sector Banks
- New Generation Private Sector Banks
- Co-operative Banks
- NBFCs

All the players were seen to be ready to enter the Retail Financial market with own merits and de-merits. However, among these players, the Foreign Banks were seen to be pro-active while they were closely followed by new generation banks. Before moving ahead, let us summarize the general understanding of the differences between Retail and Corporate Banking business which made the banks change their track.

Corporate Bank	Retail Bank
Bulk Business. Big tickets	Retail Business. Small tickets
Shrinking interest rates due to competition	Much higher spread
Business limited by geography and market	Unimaginable scope in India with 125 crores of population
High fluctuation due to Industry changing conditions	Unending market backed by Consumer goods and demand in Housing sector
Concentrated risk factor	Risk is spread across lacs of borrowers
Low cost of operations. Limited branch network	High cost of operations. (However, computerisation and alternate channels have minimised Branch banking cost)

STRUCTURAL CHANGES

While preparing for the foray in Retail arena, the foreign banks started redoing their organization structures. They realized that the prevailing pyramid structure might become a hindrance for smooth functioning of business. Overlapping of business, crossing the territories, and confusion over ownership of responsibility would have become some of the barriers for Retail business operations. This led to formation of Cylindrical structure gradually replacing the age old Pyramid concept thus creating independent business verticals like Corporate Banking, Retail Banking, SME, Treasury. To support these business verticals, other verticals were set up namely Cost Centres like Operations, Information Technology, Operations and Administration which were to function independently co-ordinating among other verticals.

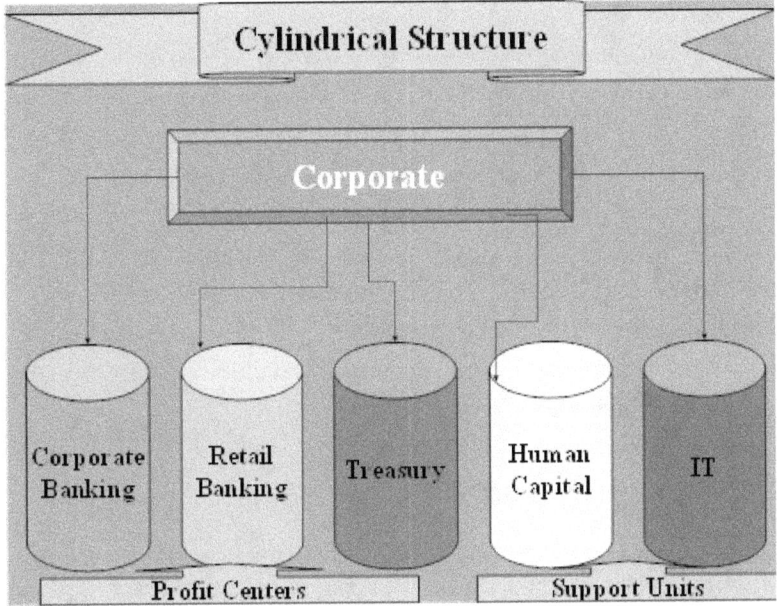

When these verticals started functioning freely and independently, there was an immense zeal and competition among Retail Banking teams in all the foreign and new generation banks to emerge with innovation and aggression driving towards tangible profitability. The support services/the cost centres also felt unchained as they were not to oblige to the Business Heads of the verticals. The top man was their referee to resolve disputes. However, during the initial years, every business vertical was in conflict with each other over business boundaries. The disputes were often to be discussed and resolved in Management Committee meetings.

Nothing could deter the journey of Retail Banking in India with its dynamic approach to the fast changing market and socio economic scenario. Gradually, the Retail Banking teams in all the banks who were recognised as proactive players in Retail Banking, took the shape in various names like Retail Banking, Consumer Banking, Personal banking. There was a massive hiring and banks started inviting walk-ins, primarily young graduates from management schools, or with engineering background or even Chartered Accountants. *I remember asking Bhanukumar, a colleague of mine in Standard Chartered Bank "Bhanu, what made you decide to join a bank with a brilliant background in Technology?" Bhanu's response was " Good question. I simply felt that working in Retail Banking in a foreign bank like this may end up being far more prospective than working as an assistant of Ratan Tata".* This was the evolution in thinking amongst bright and aspirant young generation of the later half of the 80s and it goes without saying that the catalyst was the flood of Retail Banking. This very change had essentially helped Retail Banking immensely, details of which we will come back to.

BANKS & RETAIL BANKS

Thus, at the end of the last century, the banks clearly divided into two distinct types of banks – General banks and Retail focused banks. We found that all the Nationalised banks, State Banks and its subsidiaries and co-operative banks were not in a position to decide its course of action nor were they equipped enough with technology and mind set to go for Retail Banking in the modern sense of the term. Hence they continued in their comfort zone i.e. focusing on Corporate Banking, SME sectors, Rural banking and so on within the pyramid structure. Their typical red tape culture, hesitation in decision making e.t.c also made it difficult for them against the free business culture in foreign and new generation banks where aggressive and proactive management teams had the advantage of quick decision making, freedom of thought, encouraging reward and recognition culture. The latter culture all together helped Retail Banks to move fast in the market with innovative products, branch ambience and compatible technology. As we have covered the general history of Retail Banking in India, we shall slowly start the next phase of our journey to see how the prominent players in Retail Banking got into intellectual fight with each other thus contributing to what is retail Banking today in this country.

Retail Banking Pillars

Retail Banking stands on four main pillars. These are (1) Branch Banking (2) Sales (3) Marketing and (4) Products

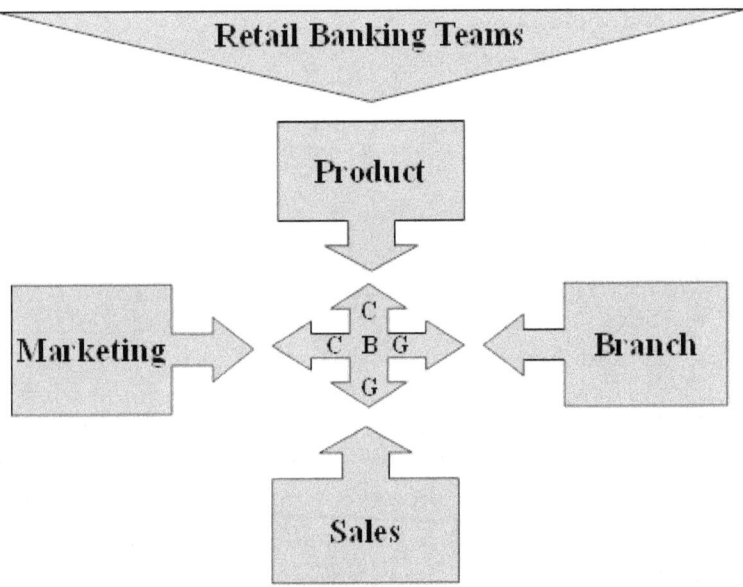

While Sales is directly and exclusively an acquisition channel, Marketing and Product are support vertical to acquisition and creation of customer base for any Retail Bank. But all activities of Retail Banking and all verticals of the group revolve round one platform. This is Branch Banking, a platform for direct interaction between bank and customers. Any Retail Bank starts with a branch first and expand over a time with growth. Hence, before moving into all activities and peripheral exercises in Retail Bank, the author trio of this book have thought of taking the readers first into the realm of Branch Banking where there is a past, a vibrant present and an exciting future with the fast advancing of technology backed by innovative bend of mind of Bankers. The main purpose of this plan is to make the read interesting in the beginning itself by pouring the first peg of Retail Banking into the goblet of Branch Banking which is the mirror or miniature of the whole.

RETAIL BANKING - IT'S FUNCTIONS

Let's start with an overview of the major functions of this vertical whether in Liabilities (Deposits) or Assets (Loans) or distribution of 3rd Party products. The major areas of Retail Banking operations are seen to rest within:

- Acquisition
- Retention
- Deepening
- Up gradation
- Referral
- Attrition
- Sales
- Distribution

Whether a customer is a depositor or a borrower, during the life time of his / her relationship with the bank, consciously or not, he / she is taken through this process in a modern Retail Bank. Before we run through the activities given above we need to have a clear understanding about the channels.

The Channels are:

1. Direct Sales channel
2. Alternate channel
3. Business Development channel
4. Affluent Market or RM channel

Let us now start with Acquisition:

ACQUISITION

As mentioned earlier, as per Retail market in India is concerned, M/s Spicer & Oppenheim, the famous UK based consultant group expressed to me, "Sky is the limit". In retrospect, what I understood was, there was nothing new in his statement. In a country with over

120 crores of population, and with a fast growing economy poising to acquire the fourth rank in global economy where else can we find a fertile Retail banking market ? But when a host of players suddenly jump into an arena to grab share of a huge market, there ought to be strategies, plans, people, product and identified fields.

When Standard Chartered had opened its doors to Retail Banking, Mr. Venkatramani and Mr. Ujwal Thacker were in the cockpit in India in the initial stage with Mr. Fred Enlow to drive from Dubai as Regional Head, Retail – Middle East and South Asia. On his visit to India, This dynamic American retail expert had made it crystal clear that 'Retail' means Number game. Prior to this, when we had started Retail Banking for Standard Chartered in India, we had to go all out in the market for bulk Deposits and Loans against Shares without paying heed to the number of people these business were garnered. I remember marketing a single loan for Rs.6 crores against shares which was highly recognised and applauded by my superiors. In fact none of the officials in newly formed Retail Bank could come out of the shadow of Corporate Banking. But Mr. Fred Enlow opened our eyes and we looked out for penetration into Mass and Mass Affluent segments driven by distributed Risk. We initially targeted the salaried individuals of renowned Corporates, established businessmen in possession of considerable amount of shares. We were selling clean overdraft facility to Salaried people and Loans against shares to business individuals. We also looked at Trusts, Clubs, Associations as soft targets for sizeable deposits. Foreign banks like HSBC, CITI, Bank of America and American Express were in the same game while the then ANZ Grindlays Bank had decided to wait and watch the progress. This is the period immediately before the new generation private banks entered the industry.

In the 90s a host of new banks had entered the market and licences were issued to them by Reserve Bank of India early in the decade. Three of these banks made foray with strong backing of financial giants like IDBI, HDFC and UTI. However, HDFC Bank was the first among these banks to proactively enter the Retail Banking arena as the banking wizard Mr. Puri was in the helm to captain the ship.

A brilliant Chartered Accountant and seasoned Corporate banker, Mr.Puri, took little time to feel the trend in the industry and he had decided to create a strong Retail franchisee which he did by inducting talents from Foreign Banks. He had placed the most costly Retail Banking icon of that time to steer Retail Banking business for HDFC Bank. Times Bank walking close to the heels of HDFC Bank started their Retail venture with Mr. Ujwal Thacker while banks like IDBI and UTI were moving slowly, may be for a bend of mind of the then Retail MDs and Board.

How right was Mr. Puri's decision, was proved in January 1998 when the industry had faced a severe liquidity crunch. Although this crisis did not last long but within the short period, may be a fortnight, banks across the soil were shaken considerably. At this point Mr. Puri decided against depending on short lived bulk deposits. He instead focussed on building a big source of low cost Retail deposits so that he could open the tap of such tank whenever he needs to without borrowing from the market. This is the background which ushered in the Product war in the days to come.

This is the period when people found all the new age banks along with foreign banks like CITI, Standard Chartered and HSBC entered the market for a quick acquisition of relationship. In this game the foreign banks were cautious about not going below the Mass Affluent market. But the new generation banks like HDFC, ICICI and the then UTI had opened their gate to mass market too. HDFC Bank was the most aggressive and they let free a big band of well trained Direct Sales force across the country for a rapid pick up of relationships and garner low cost liabilities. At this juncture, launching of Product was necessary to capture the markets thus building an ambitious customer base. CITI and other foreign banks were already actively combating each other in the product war. Now, with the new entrants in the arena, banking population started experiencing new products every now and then. Let us look at how the product war happened in Indian Retail Banking scenario.

PRODUCT WAR

Our backdrop on the stage is hung and audience are to be ready to watch the drama with the following players ready with their teams. Who are those active players? Let's have a look:

When the essential need was to acquire the maximum possible market share through penetration into targeted market segments, the answer was 'Sales'. But even in the late eighties the concept of Sales did not exist in the banking circle. At the same time the urgency for penetration beckoned for conveyor belts. The answer was 'Innovative Products' to launch. Since these first group of players were not keen on semi-urban or rural areas, their target segments were restricted to metro and tier 2 cities. Hence they started the game by launching market oriented and need based products.

Mr. Ujwal Thacker, leading the Retail team of Standard Chartered, had smelt the soil and acted swiftly. The bank came out with Executive Budget Balancer (EBB), a Personal Loan product for the salaried executives of Corporates in metro cities. It was a clean Overdraft facility to individuals and the debit balance in an account was to be liquidated by monthly salary to be credited to the borrower's account. This fast growing popularity of EBB, HSBC soon came out with almost a similar product and named it "Freedom Finance". Unlike EBB, Freedom Finance was a Term or Fixed loan where interest was to be charged on the whole amount irrespective of the utilisation requirement of the person whereas an EBB account holder had to pay interest only on the utilized fund. Needless to say, Standard Chartered took full opportunity of this flip side of Freedom Finance and dominated the new market.

Following the footsteps, ANZ Grindlays launched Cashetts almost in the same line.

On the Liability side, CITI Bank came out with a product called Unfixed Deposit, which meant that when a customer opened a Fixed Deposit (FD) account, he would be given a cheque book connected to a savings account with an overdraft limit of 75% of the value of the deposit. Whenever the customer needed a loan against deposit, he/she was not required to visit the branch. The customer had to just issue a cheque to whoever the payee was, and the cheque would be cleared through clearing on presentation. Thus a simple change in packaging a normal banking service stirred the market and people started withdrawing their existing FDs from other banks and depositing the same with CITI.

Blood beckons blood! The competition could not sit idle. This time they came out with no Me-too product but with one with added features and benefits. Standard Chartered (SCB) had launched Cluster Deposit in the form of '2 in 1. What was that? What was the value proposition in this? In the case of CITI's Cluster Deposit, if someone had to partially break a deposit, the customer was required to visit the respective branch of the bank but a customer having '2-in 1' FD of SCB only needs to issue a cheque in multiple of Rs.1000/-. On production of the cheque by the beneficiary, the instrument would be encashed. Gradually banking was becoming easy for customers. This type of deposit was replicated by the then Grindlays Bank while HSBC too eventually offered the same facility to their customers to remain at par with their competition. Much later, in the second half of the 90s, multiple new generation private sector banks entered the market with a strong Retail focus throwing challenge to the foreign banks. As a result, the product war became intense. HDFC Bank with Mr. Puri in the helm and Mr. Samit Ghosh with his talented team in the steering of Retail Bank became aggressive. At the onset of their business, HDFC Bank launched "Super Saver" – an FD product of Cluster Deposit category but coated with additional benefits and ease as offered by CITI and Standard Chartered. Going one step ahead of '2-in-1' of Standard Chartered, the Super Saver was a cluster of units of Re.1 each. This means if a depositor needed to break a sum of Rs.32,443/- from his cluster FD of Rs.1,00,000/- to make payment to someone, he was not required to break Rs.33,000/- as was in the case of other products in the same category offered by competition. He could issue a cheque of the exact amount.

HDFC Bank not only came out with the flexible Fixed Deposit account but also introduced the unique mass banking Savings product "Freedom Account" for an intensive penetration into the Mass market. What was this product? Freedom Account was a simple Savings Bank account where no minimum balance was required to be maintained. Anyone could open such savings account with a minimum entry fee of Rs.100/- and could enjoy several add-on facilities like International Debit Card, Phone Banking, Cheque book facility etc. This Freedom Account, launched on 15th August, 1997 in two branches in Kolkata, had created a ripple among the customers. At the press conference on launch, a media personality remarked "Too good to believe". This was the brain child of Mr. Samit Ghosh who has now built Ujjivan, the small finance bank.

At the end of it, we find that the whole product war emerged out of the customer psychology driving the banks to innovate "need based" products alluring the customers to use the services of the product owner. Let me give a simple example to illustrate this:

When we board any public bus on long routes, we end up meeting vendors at the terminus or when the bus stops for a longer time. These vendors on run, carry a glass jar containing assorted candies. Some of us may buy few to quench the thirst on road but many of us may refrain from buying due hygiene reasons. If the same candies are sold in an outlet with coloured transparent papers, we will not hesitate to pounce on few. This is product packaging. Mr. Samit Ghosh, the Retail Guru told me "watch the behavioural pattern of individuals, of groups, of segments. You will get solutions". It is so true as far as Retail Banking is concerned. An addition from this author - *"If you know Why is the Product, you need little to learn What is the Product. Learn the need of user segment, understand nature of the product"*.

Selling Products

With regards to products, we may look at Liability products as raw materials whereas Asset products may be considered as finished goods. The initial focus of Retails Banks should be on collecting deposits namely Current Account and Savings Account which are jointly termed as CASA. Banks need to garner enough Fixed Deposits (FD / TD). While Current Accounts are zero cost liabilities, the interest cost on Savings Bank hovers around 4 to 6%. Thus CASA, for any bank, is a low cost fund which is essential to be displayed on shelves. Against this, Term Deposits are costly with an average cost of 7.5%. CASA and TD together should not cross an average cost of 6.5% to get the advantage in the Asset Market where there are numerous Asset products for the buyers and lower the cost of fund lower the interest rates that can be offered by any bank. While drive for CASA is an activity all through the year by the bank through its various channels, marketing for Term Deposits is highly strategic and it depends on the CASA position of a bank. If CASA goes up very high, the volatility of Liability becomes a concern and a bank needs to balance these two types of deposits bringing the CASA to TD ration to an ideal 60:40 percentage.

On the basis of the cost of fund net of CRR and SLR regulated by RBI, a bank can decide to set Interest rates to offer for their multiple various asset products depending upon the offers by competition, market demand and geographical advantages or disadvantages. To build a quality asset book covering segment and geography risk is very important for a Retail bank's bottom line of the balance sheet. Profitability of an asset product majorly depends on the cost of acquisition, default percentage and cost of its collections. It also depends on segments, and city wise credit behaviour. In order to reduce cost of acquisition, the efficiency of branch platform is important since Feet on Street or Tele-callers are costs for the bank.

In this connection, the following discussion may help.

All banks offer Fixed Loan or Over Draft facility to their Deposit customers against their deposits. Banks offer a credit to the tune of 75% of the value of deposit that a customer maintains with the bank. The interest rate that is offered is at concessional rate (2.50% over the deposit rate). For some banks depending on the density of residential location, the book size of this product is considerably high. But, at the end, this is a loss making product. After taking into account the CRR / SLR the lendable surplus on a deposit is much less than 75% of the value of deposits. But banks still keep this product in the rack only to save erosion of Fixed Deposits hoping that not much people will avail themselves of the facility. Hence banks generally tend to extend loan up to 90% of the value of deposits at a commercial rate which is, of course, profitable.

We are yet to draw curtain over this chapter which will come back later in Customer Service.

SALES

Now, that we have gone through the story of Product war in Retail Banking arena, we may fasten our seat belt and step into the travelator to experience the ride through the vast field of **Acquisition**. The product innovation spree started with an accelerated speed and the urge for penetration took the northward graph. Banks felt that only the products were not enough to pull the crowd but it needed conveyor belts to push the products to the Mass in an articulated style and strategy. This was Sales – hardcore Sales. It was way back 1993 when Standard Chartered first decided to open the Sales Channel for Liability acquisition. It was also decided that two major Retail platforms – Park Street and Gariahat would be the launch pad for this venture in India. Young and thrusting Suprio Sengupta accompanied by me were given the responsibility to give the plan a shape as we two were heading the two branches respectively. When, within a fortnight or so, an outbound sales team of SCB was ready through the process of recruitment and training it marked a land mark in India's Retail Banking as the team hit the ground with the backing of a Tele-marketing team. It was the first time when acquisition of Liability was initiated by a bank through sales force in the market. Needless to say, the Sales team moved into the market with their products like "Two-in-one" and "X-chequer". This was a huge success and although other Foreign banks hesitated to go this way, few years later HDFC Bank became aggressive about Outbound Sales and they started spreading their wings with the expansion of their branch network across the country. The major weapons that HDFC Bank applied in the field for a quick mass market acquisition were Super Saver and Freedom Account. A startling result showed that in just three months, two branches of the bank in Kolkata acquired over 32000 accounts!! It was a massive and unprecedented acquisition of relationship. Most probably this was the time when Sales Force for Liability acquisition got the rubber stamp in banking industry in India. This was copied by few private sector banks but the they could not match the organized and aggressive armada of HDFC Bank.

However, this is the time when Asset products also were being sold by separate sales teams by many banks – foreign and private sector. Overall, Sale culture engulfed the Retail arena and an air of excitement propelled the growth of Retail business across industry. Let us look at how the Sales forces operated in the field :

DIRECT SALES – MODUS OPERANDI

Let's get transported to one of the most interesting field of Retail Banking which is Sales process and channels. There was no concept of 'Sales' initially. Acquisition solely depended on brand equity of the bank, reputation, ambience, and contacts. There were regular walk-ins from prospective customers based on the proximity, special services like remittances, Forex services, loans etc. Sales made an appearance in the arena with the Out Bound sales force, which was formed by the relatively aggressive banks like Standard Chartered, HDFC, ICICI and few others. The outbound sales force started knocking the doors of prospective customers with their products, plans and targets thus garnering relationships for the banks. Sales thus started through the channel that evolved first – Feet on Street which is also called as **FoS**. How is the movement of this channel?

A group of youngsters are let loose in the market after required sales and product training. They are backed by telemarketing teams operating from a central location. The Tele-marketing group generate soft and hot leads by calling people with collected database. The leads are handed over to each of the Sales people individually who connect with the interested people in order to convert the leads into business or relationships. They help the prospective customers by providing doorstep services and collect the Account Opening Documents (AOD) for further process towards opening the accounts. Once a lead is finally converted into a customer, the branches take over the relationship to further nurture this through sales of other products. However, since the lead was generated by Telemarketing and converted to Sales by FoS, the Sales person remains the contact point for some period primarily to maintain the comfort level of the customer and secondly to up-sell or cross-sell other products. We will come to the larger area of how the various channels interact among themselves with respect to customer handling and services.

MICRO/PICCO MARKET ANALYSIS

As a pre-operative process of sales there is one major activity which is called *Micro-market or Picco-market analysis*. Before hitting the ground, the command area around a branch should be mapped and customer prospects need to be analyzed. Primarily the area needs to be mapped and divided into small areas. Followed by this, all the business units, Trusts, Clubs, Associations are supposed to be identified and marked. The following two sample diagrams should explain the method:

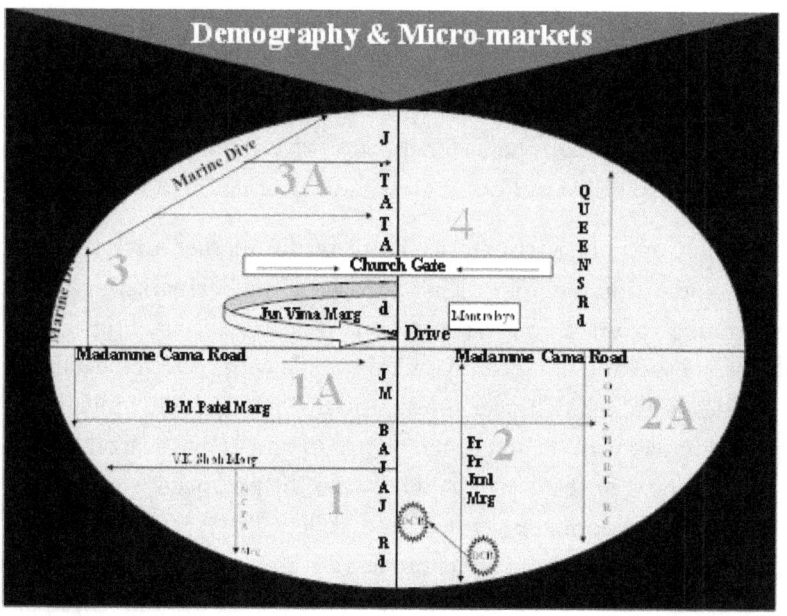

Area	Profile	Major Spots / Pockets	Opportunities
Micro / PiccoMarket Analysis			
1	Corporates &Biz Houses /Banks/Restaurants/Cultural Cntrs/Travel Agencies	Mkr Chmbrs / NCPA / Mittal Court & Chambr Chander Mukhi /Equatorial /Emiraes/Mercury / SitaTravels / Santoor /ICRA/ Foreign Missions / Banks	Salary A/cs C/Acs thru POS
1A	Corporates &Biz Houses /Banks	Vidhan Bhavan / Air India /Air Mauritous Express Towers/ Mafatlal Cntr/ GOM Qtrs	Prem C/Acs > Salary A/Cs Quality FSSA
2	Biz Hs' / Press / Corporates	Free Press Jrnl / Raheja Centr & Chmbr./ Tulsiani Chmbr / Only Paratha / MLA hostel	Salary A/cs. Hi-Val C/Acs Quality FSSA
2A	HNI Apartments / Societies / Restaurants	Indian Cancer Soc / Med Res Centre/ Mahila Vikas Mandal / Horizon /Madhusudan / Salaka / Nariman Bldgs/ Firuz Ara / Buena Vista / LIC	Prem SB A/cs Trust A/cs POS Biz > CDP > C/Ac
3	Hotels / Airlines / Restaurants	Marine Plaza / Ambassador / Hilton / Continental / Oberoi	POS Biz > Prem C/Ac with CDP
3A	HNI Apartments / Edu Insts	Mehta House/ Shanti Kutir /Shalimar/ Riviera /Yashodham/Mandara & Kedara Apts./Rakhi & Mistry Mahal. B.B.Samaj/ CCI chambers Sydenham College / Mumb univ	Prem SB A/cs & FDs Student A/Cs Priority Banking
4	Govt Offices / Political pocket / Edu Instn	Ivorine / Moonlight apts. Belvedere / Queens/ Swastik/Lily Court. MLA Qtrs/ Windsor Hs / JBIM	Priority Banking Prem SB & FD > TPD

Once the above exercise is religiously completed, the Feet on Street backed by Tele-marketing team dig out the soil and reach the target customers with the offer of right products and services. Here starts the High Trust Sales, creating confidence among prospective customers and gradually the market is penetrated.

Interestingly if Direct Sales operations and Branch operations work in tandem, it can change the Deposit mix of a bank/branch over a period of time. Initially, when a bank opens a branch in a particular area, it is the Direct Sales team who storm the market and go for a number drive by garnering relationships in thousands. The ratio of contribution from Feet on Street and Branch team starts with 80:20. As per process, these garnered relationships are handed over to the branch team for nurturing the relationship.

Eventually, the branch team and its Affluent Market wing deepen the relationship with acquired customers and thus the book value takes a steep turn. At the same time, with developed relationship, the sourcing from branch platforms increases which changes the ratio slowly and steadily coming down to 50:50. This, over years when the branch is self sufficient, slides to even 30:70 where word of mouth is a crucial contributor. Again, initially the Feet on Street garner Current and Savings accounts mainly which shoots up the CASA percentage to even 60%. Even though the cost of fund becomes attractive, this high CASA percentage gives birth to volatility of fund. This is the point when Branch platform comes into action and pushes up the Term Deposit book so that gradually the volatility of fund is reduced while the taps for low cost deposits (C/A and S/B) are ready for need. In this process, the CASA:TD percentage changes to ideal 70:30. However, more often than not, 60: 40 is more acceptable since in many PSU banks the CASA is as low as 20/25 %. Cross selling of Term deposits to Current Liability customers is a common practice and an ideal management of CASA/TD ration contributes to both low cost fund and lower volatility.

Cross selling is also done exhaustively to push Asset products to existing customers. This is very important since a branch without a strongly built asset Book has no reason for existence.

Another type of Sales is selling Third Party products where the banks sell and mutual fund products of other institutions, mainly through its branch platforms, insurance.

Asset Selling

Selling of Asset products is different ball game where Caution is a part of strategy. Here products are designed for more segment specific population considering the behavioural pattern of people from across geographies. Banks should be alert on credit history of various communities and professions. Default rate is also a major consideration. Above all, offering interest rate depends on the cost of fund that in turn is based on volatility of low cost deposits.

Asset products are directly linked to Life Style of the population where the need in life varies in stages and segments. Starting from Touch phones to cars (low model to higher ones) and housing loan, there are multiple products in the market being sold by banks, insurances and NBFCs. Pricing of these products fluctuates depending on the cost of fund and offers from competition.

Unlike Liability products, Asset Products cannot move without the support of Collection machinery. Whether in-house or outsourced, Collection machinery is an integral part of Asset business. Default rate varies from geography to geography where an individual's credit behaviour changes. Accordingly collection teams need to be pro-active. There will always be a risk in the business unless banks are selective in designing and launching their products, unless the Collection team of a bank is very efficient and are well equipped with market intelligence.

Selling 3rd Party Products

This is relatively a new chapter in the annals of Retail Bank in India. Third party products namely Life and Non-life Insurance and Mutual Fund have had made their appearance in the very beginning. The Insurance and Mutual Fund companies, as a strategy, decided to sell their products to banking customers where the market is huge and their products could be sold through banking personnel without shouldering the burden of Human Resources. Accordingly all such Insurance and Mutual fund companies who were in deep hurry to capture the pie of the market, came into contract with the banks against Commission. Not only Commission, the bank employees were offered abroad trips against performance. This brought a new wave of sales in the Retail Banking arena.

Banks started taking up ambitious to more ambitious targets month by month and left no stone unturned to achieve the same in order to increase Fee income. This became an additional allurement for the banks, especially new generation banks where the employees gave all effort to secure tickets for foreign trips.

Soon after, some banks from regional level down to front office people started miss-selling the products. The customers failed to understand this immediately and used to buy the products which had no relation to their needs. They would only realize this after around 1 or 2 years. A bank from North was identified to be involved in this practice. They got shortly merged with renowned bank who are known to be compliant. The basic trust was thus unfortunately violated.

CENTRAL PROCESSING UNIT (CPU)

For ease of rendering services, to free the business divisions from Operational hazards, to reduce Turn Around Time, to increase efficiency and accuracy and finally to reduce Cost of Operations, Retail Banks started a new division which is essentially a back office under Operations where all account opening activities and associated functions like Cheque book delivery, Account closing etc were under this centralized operations unit. While primarily this new system created some uneasiness among bankers, over a period of time this became an integral part of Retail Banking. Other business units like Corporate Bank, Investment Bank and Treasury also benefitted out of this support service.

Let us see how Central Processing Unit functions. After a sales officer contacts a prospective customer and the deal is closed, the customer completes all Account Opening Documentations (AOD) and returns to the Sales officer who, in turn, submits the same to the related branch. From here, the set of AOD after due screening is sent to CPU. The officers at CPU check and ensure that AODs are in order in all respect. This exercise is followed by opening the account in system. In the next step, Cheque book and Welcome kit are sent directly to the customer who is supposed to activate the ATM /Debit card and start operating the account. CPU thereafter is responsible for safe keeping the documents and other records whether the relationship is live or dormant. If an account is closed, the branch sends the request to CPU who close the account in system after due verification of papers.

This centralization of account opening and maintenance was another landmark in the wake of Retail Banking in India. After initial hesitation and few confusions, the Retail Banks found this change easy while CPU, under Operations, is a platform independent of business units hence not under obligation to entertain business units' wishes which do not conform to regulatory or ethical guidelines. The following diagram may help to take a glance at how Business and CPU work in a tandem. However, both back and front office got a revolutionary support from the huge development in IT sector. Let's take a quick glance :

The purpose of Banking for people, long before it was called Retail Banking, was to provide an organized platform to cater to the three broad needs: safe-keeping of money when one has surplus, be able to borrow money when they fall short of it and transfer money in lieu of goods or services. As the practice grew into an industry these three needs became the major disciplines and came to be known as Deposits, Loans and Payments respectively.

While processes, laws and technology have revolutionized all disciplines of banking through the ages, we see a radical transformation in the way Payments have evolved, especially in the past few decades. To appreciate the evolution of technology in payments we must remind ourselves that Technology exists to serve business and to help it achieve outcomes. In the case of payments, the expected outcomes are A. Speed of Transfer and B. Convenience of making a payment – anytime, anywhere.

Payments have been made since the introduction of currency in the society and the technology of those times that enabled currency introduction was the processes used in Mints to create coins. But for the scope of this book, let us limit our discussion to Information Technology encompassing the use of electronics and data.

The first game-changing move from the perspective of IT in Banking Payments came with the digitization of journals at the Clearing Houses. A clearing house is a regulated intermediary that facilitates the settlement process between two financial institutions. When a payment is made by Party A which holds an account with Bank X to a Party B which holds an account with Bank Y. This means money must move from Bank X to Bank Y while the ledgers of Party A and Party B in their respective banks are updated with the correct numbers. The original practices required representatives of the banks to convene at the clearing house with the promising notes (e.g. cheques or banker's drafts) and update their books of accounts. The process would take 2-3 days if in the same town before the recipients account started showing the received money. The practice came to be known as

T+2 Payment, which takes 2 days from the date of Transfer (or making the payment).

They say Necessity is the Mother of Invention. I would add that perhaps "the strive for increased convenience is the mother of the continuous improvement and evolution of technology". Due to the sheer volume of transactions and the need to keep records accurate, Banking sector was the first to harness the power of Charles Babbage's invention of electronic computers. Soon after individual bank records became digital, the cumbersome clearing house book-keeping were replaced by data entry into connected machines that would settle the bank accounts.

Since then there was no looking back. The process of clearing today runs on APIs (Application Programming Interface) that connects banks electronically and exchange data on payments. Physical representation is no more required in the Clearing Houses and they are known as Automated Clearing Houses. While bulk of the payments are triggered through electronic channels like internet banking portals, mobile apps etc., promissory notes like Cheques and Drafts that were exchanged in Clearing Houses are now shared as an image from the receiving bank over these API connectors as a proof of payment. The T+2 wait for the recipient is now reduced to near real-time if the parties had executed a prior transaction. It takes about a day for first time transactions between two parties.

Global payment, on the other hand, is enabled by SWIFT (Society for Worldwide Interbank Financial Telecommunication). This was a uniform protocol of exchanging payment information over secured lines across financial entities around the world. The efficiency of Global payments and settlements is also now near real-time. Be it bank to bank payments or using an intermediary like Western Union Money transfer, the amount is credited within minutes after the transfer is triggered.

Direct Sales – Flow Chart

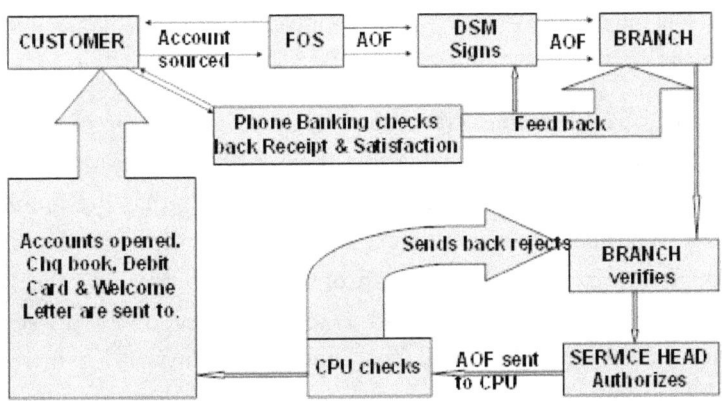

Centralization of processing, in fact, brought a remarkable change in banking in the light of Checks and Control. This brought independence in operations without overlooking inter or intra dependency. In this system, Business units cannot exercise pressure on Operations to compromise with regulatory strictures. This helped to maintain of relationships.

While the main purpose of resorting to the relatively newer channel called Direct Sales or Feet on Street was to penetrate into Mass and Mass Affluent markets and expand the reach, the bank also needed to think about the cost of acquisition. The Feet on Street operate in the field primary to:

ALTERNATE CHANNELS

Before we peep through the window of **Retention**, which is a crucial part of Retail banking activities, we must look at various channels that were launched in phases reducing branch activities. Since Retail Banking means people or huge number of customers as opposed to other verticals of banking, the branch banking part started feeling the heat of customer rush in the branch premises with the acquisition spree. The cost of servicing customers was rising with forced increase of manpower and branch space. So the need of keeping the customers away from branches was strongly felt and this gave birth to Alternate Channels as *"necessity is the mother of invention"*.

Let me give an example - Mr. Robinson thinks of throwing a party in his three BHK flat on the occasion of his 50th marriage anniversary. When he chalks out his list of invitees, he finds that the number hits a minimum of 125 which can be forcefully brought down to 100. Now, Mr. Robinson has two options. He can call all the 100 heads to his flat which will lead to a pandemonium due to acute space constraint. There will be a high possibility of his invitees bad mouthing when they leave. Alternatively, Robinson can send sweets and delicious food, appropriate packaged and professionally delivered, to the invitees who will then send wishes or blessings to the Robinsons.

Similarly, with the increasing pressure on branch premises due to unmanageable footfall of customer following Retail Bank's drive to garner as many relationships as possible in the shortest time, the banks exploring to introduce alternate channels to service their customers outside the limited space of branch premises. Thus, with time, starting with ATMs, an array of channels became a reality in Indian banking industry. Let us take a glance:

1. Automated Teller Machine (ATM)
2. Point of Sales (POS) terminals where Debit / Credit Cards are used
3. Credit Cards
4. Phone Banking
5. Mobile Banking
6. Internet Banking

At the same time, the customer world finds a massive development in technology ushering in quick fund transfer, payment system,

Management Information System (MIS) and so on. A spate chapter is devoted to transport the readers to update on the latest and future of technology in banking across the globe bringing revolution hitherto thought of.

These channels, though primarily are meant to service the customers at various points, take part in acquiring new relationships as well. While phone Banking is a direct contributor in this activity, ATMs and Internet banking play a pivotal role through advertising products and services to attract the customers.

Servicing through Alternate Channels

Alternate Channels are essentially the blessings of technology. While this area of services divert the customers from branch premises thus reducing rush and cost of operations, it is imperative for a bank to ensure that customers receive uninterrupted services from those mechanical interfaces where they do not have any opportunity to lodge their grievances with human desks over shortfall in services. At points like ATMs, Point of Sales (POS) customers will not appreciate high downtime. In general, customers have patience but it cannot be taken for granted. If high downtime continues to be a frequent problem, customers will leave. Hence Downtime should not be less than 99.50 % by all means.

Alternate channels are a revolution in banking industry. It has not only reduced Cost of operation, it has reduced pressure on the branch banking channel thus helping directly in enhancing service quality over the counter. Let us take a live situation as under:

RETENTION

This is the most important area as regards Customers of the bank. It's easy to acquire new customers displaying innovative products and alluring them with attractive features with tangible benefits - financial or non-financial. But the real challenge lies in retaining those customers and increasing their value with the bank. A customer enters the bank with a certain amount of expectation in respect of Services involving Turn Around Time (TAT), Accuracy, Service Quality and all. The expectation also involves personal interaction. This is Service and Personal Touch. Reading customer psychology and understanding the customer is absolute must to retain them.

There are customers who voice their dissatisfactions even in public and a reactive management of the situation can bring those individuals under control. But there are many who are reluctant to talk of their bad experiences in public. They rather prefer to silently separate themselves from their banker as the market is open to choice. Thus, in the unawareness of the bank, dissatisfied customers slowly walk away and gradually there is an erosion of customer base, may be most valuable chunk of the base. As a result, not only other existing customer may exit, this also becomes a hindrance for new acquisition as the reputation of the bank takes a hit.

This is where comes the Service Quality.

SERVICE QUALITY

While a customer is attracted to a bank for need based products, interest rates and accessibility to branch network, they stay back only for Service Quality. With the delight and convenience of banking, customers not only continue with a bank, their "Feel Good" factor gets translated into their Repeat Purchase and they get deeply associated with the bank over a period of time. Hence, the main activity after acquisition of an individual customer and also after building a considerable customer base, is to make the customers feel good and to retain them, thus deepening the relationship with time. Let us examine what sre the ways to keep the customers happy.

Layout of Branch Premise : While thinking of Retail Banking one must, time and again, keep in mind that Retail Banking essentially deals with human psychology, behavioural pattern of an individual. A branch layout also plays an important role. Let me give an example how human psychology forces an individual to behave in a pattern. If one visits a branch premise of a Public Sector bank, one generally faces the Cash Counter immediately after entering the hall. He, then, crosses the chest height counters to reach human faces for work other than cash transaction. Again, at the entrance itself one will invariably come across the collapsible gate drawn half way from both sides and then chained with a lock keeping maximum two feet space for a customer to slip in. The logic is, in case of attempt of burglary, the burglars won't be able to take in or out the big boxes. Hilarious though, this is the age old practice which cannot be argued.

On the other hand, in case of Foreign or New Generation banks, the picture is different and the difference comes from outlook, concept and understanding human psychology driven by knowledge of Retail Banking. The entrance of a new generation or foreign bank is wide open with transparent glasses enabling anyone to look through inside the hall. In place of high counters, there are tables for effective interface with customers. The cash counters are set almost at the end of the hall giving a "wide open" effect. This too has a relation with the mindset of a person - An open hall lends a different feeling to a customer as juxtaposed to a cluttered banking area. Additionally, many of the branch premises of modern banks give a showroom effect where it looks like a Financial Mall. Signage have become another important feature in such banks where customers self direct themselves to the destination point to get their work done.

I remember, once a young Retail Banking head of an upcoming new generation bank set an interesting tag line for the bank as "Indian flavour, but international service". Shortly the bank had change of guard when the new MD from CITI bank commented " what Indian flavour ? flavour of liquor from Chai Bharh (earthen pot to serve tea) ?" In fact when the surge of Retail Banking have already hit the shore of this sub-continent and the effect is reaching far in new Avatar, a bank should be cautious about how it builds its image. Customers' mindset varies from segment to segment, place to place and we need to keep in mind their behavioural reactions.

SELECTION OF BRANCH NETWORK

Selection of branch location is of paramount importance in ensuring future business. I remember, a new generation bank during the nineties had adopted a novel strategy. They had decided to open their branches in premises next to or very near by a PSU bank branch It really worked when there were outflow of customers from the neighbouring PSU bank branch simply because, ambience, technology and modern approach to banking. Hinterland strategy does also play an important role. Banks need to carefully identify the areas or pockets which are lowly banked or even unbanked. In a major part of the country people still need banking facilities. Even potential areas are unbanked. In this condition banks need to adopt hinterland strategy and create foot prints where competition is negligible or manageable. First entrant has always an advantage with local studies of population, lifestyle, business presence etc. Again, a micro/picco market analysis helps in capturing the pockets and create market share.

TO SUM UP:

- Careful selection of location.
- To be given shape of a financial mall.
- To be devoted to Sales & X-sales backed by ideal after-sales service.
- To create favorable word of mouth.
- Retention and Up gradation – a major role.
- Effective Footprints across the country.

At the end of it how a branch should be, depends upon combination of multiple factors as below:

- Customer friendly layout of the branch
- Quality of product, its features and benefits
- Delivery of the products
- Ambience and Feel Good factor in the premises
- Customer Service
- After Sales Service

I remember, before opening the second branch of HDFC Bank's branch in Kolkata in early 1997, my Retail Banking Guru told me "How you build your franchisee depends on you. Decide, whether you make the platform a McDonald or K.C.Das' Rasgullah shop. Both are famous but there is difference in class". Something to learn from this advice.

CUSTOMER SERVICE & SATISFACTION

Customers look for their needs to be satisfied and they are critical about the various products and services offered by different banks. This includes financial return as well. As we have discussed the product war among banks to get the better of other always, a bank needs to ensure that their products are "need based" ones and are easy to understand and handled by the customers who are not on the same platform as per intellectual level is concerned. Hence, the very nature of the product should be segment specific with transparency, market competitive and of course offers tangible return. At the same time, it is important to keep in mind that a customer does not switch loyalty only for few basic points of difference. In this, Personal Touch plays a pivotal role creating a positive impact upon customers. While technology has taken Bank services to an unimaginable height, Personal Touch speaks the last word. A heart to heart communication with eye contacts generates Trust which is the last word in Customer Service. When a customer builds relationship with a branch of a particular bank, it does not matter to him whether the person in the front desk catering his need is a bright young personality with smart English pronunciation and well taught courtesy. He rather will prefer a bald headed middle aged person with knowledge, smile, calmness and accuracy because his need is Financial where he needs to depend on someone truly dependable.

A quick disposal of a customer may be one of the very basic requirements that any individual look forward to. Modern Banks have introduced Token system which is good as a systematic approach to the solution but end of it, human hands must act fast. There was a Front Line staff in the then Grindlays Bank. He was known as Raj. My father was a regular visitor to Jodhpur Park branch where Raj used to work. All on a sudden Grindlays declared VRS (in fact CRS) for their staff and Raj was one of the victims of time. One day my father had called me to his room and instructed me to accommodate him in IDBI Bank where I was working. He explained that for any small to big service, his go-to person was only Raj and he received a single window service in no time. Moreover, he was moved with his ever smiling face. What I am trying to communicate is, a front line staff should build a relationship with a customer like this through his services so that the customer can go to the extent of saving his job. It's a one to one relationship which is more than a bondage for which a customer does not switch loyalty for small benefits.

Another important area is to understand the customers' preferred banking time. The whole of the day is ideal but surely not practical. Some banks are found to introduce split banking hours with recess of few hours in between. This often brings drudgery among the staff members for working long hours. People frequently advocate Sunday banking for whole day. But if we look at the Lifestyle of an individual, we find that a person often prefers to complete the banking related works during the first one or two hours from 10 am on Sundays and likes to idle away time in the noon whereas the evenings are utilized in socializing. Hence half-day on Sundays are found suitable. This is how we should address the banking transaction timing for the customers taking into consideration, their life style.

The whole of Retail Bank is based on human psychology and Life Style of people and banks need to understand the same. The following two examples may be a bit interesting:

When a person stands at the edge of a broad and busy road to cross it and if he has two options — foot bridge and under pass, he will, by all probability, choose the under pass since to his mind the easiness to climb down the stairs of the under pass will appear easier. The fact that after touching the underground, he will have to climb will not cross his mind. Whereas if he crosses by the foot bridge, he needs to climb first but once he reaches the top, he will have the comfort of climbing down. In both ways the same exercise is involved but psychology is a different aspect altogether.

Sanjay Babu, a retired individual, is suffering from severe pain in the knee since the last four years. He goes to vegetable market thrice a week. There are two big vegetable vendors placed next to each other. Both are equally equipped commodities and both possess commendable selling skills with cordiality. But surprisingly Sanjay Babu buys vegetables from one particular vendor only. When probed with Sanjay Babu, the following came out:

Sanjay Babu had developed acute Osteoarthritis in his right keen over the last decade and was suffering for that. It was difficult for him to stand in a place for some time. The vendor from whom he buys his vegetable keeps two stools in front of his stall whereas there is no such thing provided by the other vendor. Sanjay Babu prefers to buy his stuff sitting in a place so that his knee does not pain him. This is a simple touch that tells of the basic of customer service. This is understanding your customer well which will build the difference.

Again, while the bank may and generally does decide the standard of Delivery, rather Customer Service, the Customer Satisfaction is always defined by the customers only. Hence determination of Service quality should start from customers and not from the bank. If a customer does not get the satisfaction they look for, there is something wrong with the bank's understanding of the customer or the segment.

Some more areas in Customer Service, if not mentioned, will leave the discussion incomplete.

Some Observations :

1. Studies show that customers tell twice as many people about a bad experience as they speak about a good one.
2. A typical dissatisfied customer will narrate 8 to 10 people about his / her problem.

3. 7 out of 10 complaining customers will engage with you again if you resolve the complaint in their favor.
4. If you resolve a complaint on the spot, 95% of complaining customers will be retained.

Eye Opener:

1. It's easier to get present customers to buy 10% more, than to increase your customer base by 10%.
2. Firms selling services depend on existing customers for 85 – 95% of their business.
3. Industry experts say superior customer service in stores is crucial with the rising popularity of catalogues, home shopping networks and other Retail formats that offer discount prices.

To Think Of :

1. 80% of successful new product & service ideas come from customer ideas.
2. It costs six times more to attract a new customer than it does to keep an old one.
3. According to the National Customer satisfaction index, customer satisfaction with goods and services declined in 1995.

Post acquisition, retention of customers is an ongoing process. Banks need to invest in terms of skilled and committed human resource as well as technology which, in turn generates delight in customers. This is a cycle that must go on.

There must be a continuous process of identifying the gaps between the customers' expectation and what actually the bank offers. At the same time, the bank's existing infrastructure got to be assessed and if there is any shortfall, that gap needs to be covered by enhancing the facilities, thus, business comes, when matched with the expectations of customers.

A Reality

It's a sad reality that grievances regarding Customer Service have become part and parcel. Whether bankers of yester years or gray hair customers, a majority of population is being found sceptical about the quality of customer service. A general observation points fingers more to the lack of appropriate training and grooming of the employees, making them ready to create delight for the customer.

The gap is both at the knowledge and attitudinal area which are often being neglected by the banks and people are deployed without ensuring they are ready for the job. More often than not, customers get frustrated because there is a significant lack of banking related knowledge on part of the staff. For instance, a Fixed Deposit is in the joint names of two persons with the mandate "Either or Survivor". On demise of one person when the survivor approaches the bank to withdraw the amount on maturity, he is told that the amount cannot be given without signature of the other person (who is dead). Hilarious indeed!! This is the result of imparting a crash course to the employees in a hurry expecting that the person will learn on-the-job. This is uncalled for. A group of motivated and educated employees can keep their customers happy only if they are backed by rigorous training in areas of Banking rules and regulations, IT as well as Customer Service.

However, in order to become a truly customer friendly bank, the following are to be incorporated in the Rule Book:

1. Banks should be sincerely responsive to the customers. Response to enquiries against advertisement is the first hand impression. The responses should be quick creating interest in the prospective customer.
2. Listen to Customers. This is the gateway to understand the need of the customer and thus provide resolution. Patience hearing creates pleasure and confidence in the customer about the banker on the other side of the table.

3. Being helpful is another requirement. The body language needs to create a positive impression in the customer about the person he is dealing with.

4. Lodging Complaints should seem to be easy to the customer. It is an essential route to gather input to boost customer satisfaction. Although many people do not complain. Once a complaint is received, it needs to be responded before long. If immediate resolution is difficult, a holding reply should reach the customer assuring him that the matter is being addressed and the bank will soon get back to him.

5. The complaint from the Customer must be analysed and the incidents must be probed. Bank then should resolve the problem of the customer and provide the solution to him.

6. Customers need to be respected, especially customers with vintage who are treated to be assets to the bank. They should be kept happy.

7. No advertisement on Bill Board, Newspaper or in any other media works as the Word of Mouth does. Hence it is crucial to keep customers happy. One satisfied customer tells ten individuals about his experience. This works like magic. A happy customer is the strongest Ambassador of the bank.

8. Being nice with a customer is not enough. While listening to a customer, dealing with him or understanding his problem, it is necessary to be nice to him inflicting a sense of easiness to him. But this is not the end and the bank should not suffer from satiety. Niceness is only a process in handling a customer and not enough since a Customer wants result and not a smiling face only.

Hence a relationship is not to be taken granted always. Unless a customer is from the bank, he may switch over to competition. In this process he may continue with a bare minimum value relation with his existing banker and silently move his transactions to greener pastures.

Periodical tracking of individual customers or group of customers is to be done religiously and whenever a customer exits, the bank must find out why. Unavoidable attrition is bound to happen if the root cause of exit of a customer or a group is not identified, analysed and corrective measures are taken.

The short paragraph on Deepening below may help on how to go about it.

DEEPENING

Let us take an example as under to examine:

A group of Savings Bank relationships acquired in the 1st Quarter of 2018													
Acquired: Jan to Mar'18		As on 30/6/18		As on 30/9/18		As on 31/12/18		As on 31/3/19		As on 30/6/19		Incr/ Decr	
No	Value	No	Value	No	Value	No	Value	No	Value	No	Value	No	Value
1718	31675	1715	32549	1699	43211	1532	54765	1530	33567	1498	67002	-320	35327

The above MIS shows that a branch garnered from the market 1718 Savings relationships during the first quarter of 2018 with an initial aggregate value of Rs.31675/-. In June, the same year three accounts were closed in natural process but the value increased to Rs.32549/-. Hence there is no erosion. At the end of the following quarter we see the branch losing 16 relationships. However, there is an increase in value to Rs.43211/-. The branch needs to look at the reasons of exit of 16 customers. As on December 31st, we note with concern that the branch lost 33 relationships. Is it because of dissatisfaction, closure of salary accounts of a small company, or anything else? Although the value of the total went up to Rs.54765/=, the branch management should not sleep satisfied because value may play volatile. Around March end, there is a slide in value to Rs.33567/-. We witness a negligible amount of attrition. This may be due to year-end Tax liabilities of individuals. As on June 30th, we find the value has doubled, with an attrition of 32 customers. Thus in a year, a branch increased its savings bank value by over Rs.35000/- but lost from the said group of 18% relationships which is not comfortable for the branch.

If the reason for exit of the 320 customers is a common dissatisfaction over services, features or benefits or indifference in treatment, then it surely affects other customers too who will also exit or have already switched loyalty. Mere increase in value of relationships cannot be a point of satisfaction. It's to be remembered that Retail is always a Number game where number generates Value. Hence erosion in Number has to be taken seriously. A low value customer is not necessarily a person of low net worth. Who knows, he does not maintain a hefty amount with other bank and he stepped on a new platform to test the Service? Exit Interview is thus crucial and has to be conducted in case of every customer severing relationship with the bank. Simply by retaining a customer bank's job does not end. The relationship is to be nurtured in such a way that over a period of time the relationship between the customer and the bank blooms in value and profitability.

So, Deepening is an important exercise for any bank-branch with a focused approach and MIS needs to be used as a tool in this effort. But how well can Deepening be done and what are the exercises to be followed religiously? Let's talk to our Customers who are primarily and essentially mortal human beings with all their human traits like sentiments, sense of insecurity, patience/ impatience, time conscious. So, what do they expect, especially from a bank where they have established relationship very recently?

DELIVERY –

First impression matters. After establishing a new relationship with a new bank, a customer expects the Account Opening Kit containing cheque book, Debit card, Deposit slips and other papers delivered within less than a week delivered at doorstep. It is needless to say that the Passwords to Alternate channels should follow before long so that the customer starts banking operations when the initial relationship starts.

The customer kit that is delivered after opening the account should create a good impression. The papers inside the envelope should explain everything about the deliverables by the bank and everything that the customer can expect from the bank.

CONTACT –

Once the banking relationship starts, it's important to establish contacts with the consumer primarily over phone and mails (physical or electronic) and ideally when the customer personally visits the branch for any purpose. He / she should be brought to awareness about the various products and services of the bank and the features/benefits that the customer can enjoy. In this process, over a period of time, customers should ideally be inducted as part of the bank's extended family. In the meantime, the Customer Profile should be ready with available information and also with whatever information can be gathered about his / her relationships with other banks, if any. This information may be effectively used to explore the need of a customer and to identify the right product for him. Next step is to go through a sales process to establish rapport with the person, to bring him to confidence and then provided him the solution, and not simply offer him the product.

The contact point to the customers may be many such as, the Personal Banker or Customer Service officer at the branch, the Direct Sales officer who brought him to the bank or the Tele-servicing executive. As time goes and the relationship deepens Trust and Value, the bank may examine the nature of the progress and if found feasible and considerably prospective, a Relationship Manager may be engaged to take the bonding to higher level with array of benefits. The thumb rule is, a customer should ideally be locked with a minimum of two and half products, Asset, Liability or Third Party to make the relationship financially viable. In short, a new customer should be converted into a Profitable Relationship through constant touch and sales efforts.

SALES

What follows next is Sales, backed by Marketing. A Customer, psychologically, loves it if the bank gets in touch with him or her every now and then across platforms. There should be a decent bombardment of calls, brochures and mails informing the customers of new products, new services, any change in FD or loan rates etc to keep the customers away from competition and engaged with the bank and bank's personnel.

While this process is on, Sales will be a simultaneous and ongoing activity ensuring that a customer is locked with the bank with at least two and half product on an average thus contributing to the bottom line of the bank's balance sheet. How? A multi pronged attack is the best way to higher strike rate. When one Sales Team hunts for Deposit accounts from the customers, the others push asset products and with little loss of time the Branch people sell Insurance, mutual fund and all generating spot income for the bank. The purpose is to ascertain that a sizable income is generated from a customer through all the products sold. We will discuss this part more in details when we enter the Priority or Privilege Banking zone. Let the basics be set right before making ambitious and sophisticated ventures.

As a process, for any branch, the initial sales for mass market should be done by the Feet on Street. On careful mapping of the area, the Relationship Managers should knock the potential customers in the command area as well as filtering the acquired relationships by Direct Sales team and to contact the potential customers from that chunk. As regards high potential individuals and institutional accounts, it should be the responsibility of the Branch Head (and sometimes, Regional Head) to tap these sources taking the Relationship Manager in the exercise so that once such customers are introduced, the relationship management can be handed over to the Relationship Manager of the branch.

At Branch level, following are the sales activities:

- Acquisition – getting in a new customer
- Cross selling – selling him an additional product
- Deepening – acquiring higher wallet share of the customer in the same product
- Referencing – acquiring new customers through existing customers
- Recall – Building the brand in customer's mind

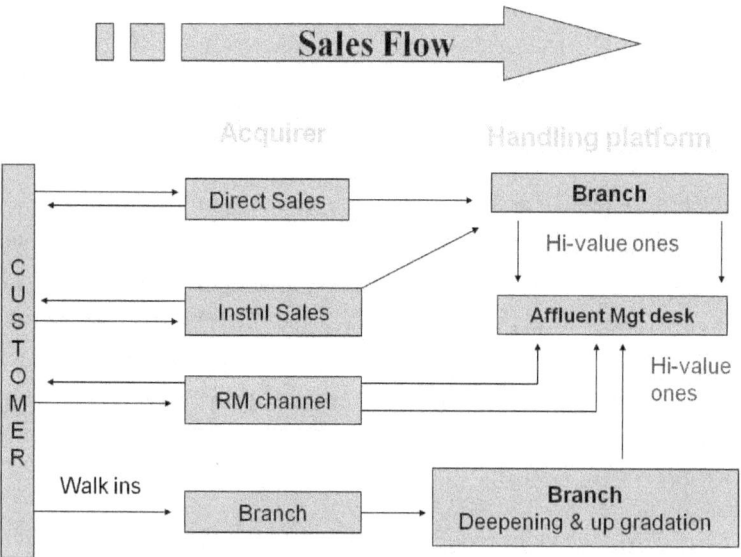

The above diagram may illustrate how all the sales channels namely, Direct Sales, Branch platform and Relationship Management should work hand in hand to garner relationship and enhance the total value of the book.

Some in-branch activities can be summed up as below:

- Referral program
- HNW meet
- Periodic campaigns
- Product champions

- Product specific RMs for specific branches
- Periodic training of front office branch staff
- Telemarketing – for deepening

Referral Program

Referral Program is a low cost acquisition route for the bank. It's actually a Customer Get Customer plan where each existing customer is impressed upon to refer new relationship to the bank. This helps increasing the customer base at lowest cost and on the other hand KYC formalities are easier than in the case of totally unknown persons.

HNW Meet

When we travel through the top end customer segment and their behavior, we will understand how important it is to retain and deepen the bonding. Generally for any branch or any cluster of branches, High Net Worth customer meet is very important given the psychology of this segment. Again it relates to the lifestyle of the top end segment of the customers. What they want is recognition from their bank that they are different from the mass and are treated differently. (The author once had a discussion with one of his relative who was a rich businessman. During the discussion, multiple times, he mentioned that every year he is invited by HSBC to their HNW meet. There was an obvious pride in his voice). This is the psychology of HNW segment which needs to be shown required respect. Often these meets lead to increasing the book value and also acquiring new customers through referrals.

Periodic Campaigns

I am allured to talk about Campaigns in the field. It has a small history where I was emotionally involved. Periodic campaigns are carried on by Direct Sales teams for speedy acquisition of customers towards accelerated growth of the book. This Direct Sales for

Liabilities was heralded by Standard Charted bank and pioneered by Suprio Sengupta and myself in India market starting from Kolkata. Such campaigns were usually conducted for a day or two in a specific locality, adequately mapped, where a band of Feet on Street used to make cold calls at door steps and inviting the household to open relationship with the bank. These teams were divided into multiple groups who used to work from dawn to dusk in their allotted pockets. We used to announce prize money for individuals and groups for performances. All of them used to assemble at day end in a place or in the local branch to celebrate achievement. There was excitement in team work and bank used to penetrate in the markets smoothly with their products.

Training of Front Office Staff

For any modern Retail Bank, ongoing training of front line staff is an unavoidable priority. Technology changes, new products are launched, old products are upgraded and interest rates are changed throughout the year. The front line staff who regularly interface with customers, need to be refreshed with the knowledge of such development. Failure to adhere to this, leads to incomplete information and confuse the customers, who eventually lose trust in the bank. It thus necessitates refreshment of current knowledge of the staff members and skill them to cope up with time.

Telemarketing

Telemarketing personnel at branch level or at central locations are active in keeping regular touch with customers handling their complaints, service needs and for opening new accounts towards deepening the customer books. This is an ongoing and daily activity which should be adequately planned, driven and monitored for desired result. Telemarketing is thus a strong tool to keep in regular touch with customers at all levels and to feel their pulse in respect of their perception about their banker.

High Trust Sales

Selling and Trust hold equal importance so far a customer is concerned. A sale is never complete until Trust is totally dissolved in it. A customer generally approaches a bank not merely to buy a product but to get an advice – a financial solution that he needs. Here comes the role that is important, of the Banking personnel. At this stage the Personal Banker is expected to be a patient listener. Upon hearing out and analysing the need of the customer, the bank must arrive at a solution. This solution must be an honest one and to the best interest of the Customer who should go back with better comfort and enhanced Trust in the bank. It is a cyclic order where a customer gets satisfied with the bank and returns with further business. Thus a bank grows with its satisfied and loyal customer. Coming to the Trust associated with Selling a story below may help to understand it better.

During the second half of the nineties a mariner stepped in my room with his wife and daughter. This time I was heading the region at HDFC Bank. This gentleman was long known to me being a neighbour and recently retired with a good amount of related benefits. He asked my advice on where to place a crore of money in Fixed Deposit. Since our Term Deposit rate was considerably lower than what was being offered by UTI (presently AXIS Bank), I advised him to place his fund with Axis Bank. As it is for HDFC Bank, there was little or no interest in high cost deposit. However, my advice was a surprise to this retired mariner who expected me to request him to keep his deposit with my bank. When I told him that Axis Bank was offering higher FD rate, he was silent for some time. I requested him to open a Savings account with HDFC Bank and to have a taste of our service. He left with required forms. A week later he appeared and not only opened a Savings account but placed the fund in Fixed Deposit with HDFC Bank only. He said "For a difference of one per cent I will not leave you guys". This is possibly creating Trust in a Customer.

- We buy from people we trust, people we like.
- Successful people don't sell price. They sell Value.
- Selling is actually providing.
- Establishing Trust takes time and sometimes that means adding value without receiving business.
- Sales happen as a result of trust – higher the Trust, greater is the Sale.

Selling is always a process which needs to be followed in order to build Trust in the mind of the prospective or existing customer. Once the trust is built, selling a product will be a cake walk. However, before approaching customer we should note why people buy:

1. Status symbol
2. Love and care
3. Curiosity
4. Imitation
5. Fear of non-possession
6. Rivalry
7. Self preservation

It is, therefore, crucial to probe and understand the need of the customer and the purpose of his buying the product. A simple yet religious route needs to be followed as under:

- ➢ Contact the customer and ask for a time, convenient to him, for a meeting.
- ➢ After scheduling the appointment, meet him well prepared.
- ➢ Interview the person, probe, and try to fathom his basic value needs and lead to highest value need.
- ➢ Provide him with a solution to his need. Ensure that the provided solution meets the highest need of the customer and also the core value of the need is fulfilled.
- ➢ At the final step ask the customer whether he is satisfied with the solution. If the response is affirmative, it is better to reconfirm his satisfaction.
- ➢ Once the above steps are completed, softly ask for business.

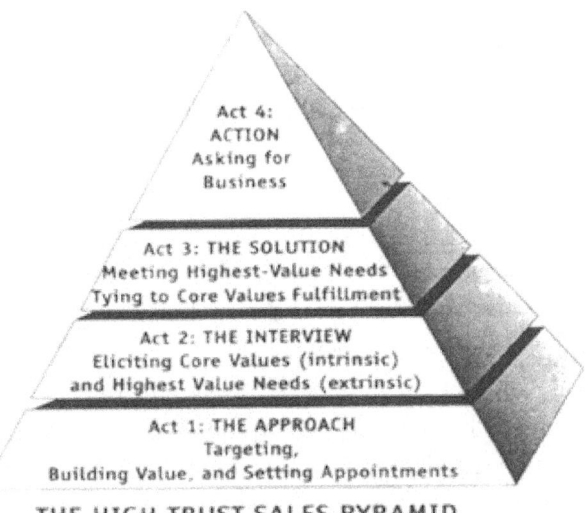

THE HIGH TRUST SALES PYRAMID

In spite of whatever is written above about the sales process or customer need, one important area is still to be to be touched and that is Selling Skill but for which the above efforts remain fruitless. For this, a Sales person needs adequate training and the right mind set to sell. This is because in banking industry we often find people who are averse to Sales, the reason mostly is a fear to lose. Following chart may explain this:

Why RMs Fail

POOR IN	LACK OF	OTHERS
Planning	Continuous Training	Procrastination
Attitude	Specific Goals	Neglecting self Evaluation
Use of time	Self Discipline	Inability 2 cope with Rejection
	Concentration	Inability 2 fail
	Creative imagination	

SERVICE - After Sales

We have discussed Delivery, Personal Touch and Sales. But the most important part is **After Sales Service** but for which Retention of customers remains in dream and all plans, all strategies and execution will go in vain resulting in huge loss of investments and time. It is easy, by gift of the gab and sales skills, to attract and invite customers to the bank but it's a big challenge to retain the personality. This is possible only through successful After Sales Service and constant Personal touch. When customers board a bank's platform, they come with certain hope and expectation which they want to experience in reality. It's the sole responsibility of the bank to make sure that it happens. Fall in service standard leads to gradual erosion in customer base where the exits are silent and there is a gradual drift of soil from under the feet.

What is also essential is to keep a regular connect with the customers once the relationship is established. Tele-marketing is one effective way. This humanotronic (human + Electronic) channel which plays a big role in sourcing new customers need to continue the touch post opening the account. This process helps in understanding the customers' way of mind with respect to post relation experience.

Satisfaction of a customer post opening accounts with a bank attracts Repeat Purchase. Customer is a human being with all human elements. One of these is sensitivity. If found neglected, the customer will become indifferent and will drift away from the bank. However, a little ego massaging, making him feel important, will help in extracting more value from the customer to the benefit of the bank.

UPGRADATION

After crossing the milestones of Acquisition, Retention and Deepening, it's important to get an idea about the arena of Up Gradation. During the acquisition spree and the process of holding back the acquired relationships, banks often leave behind some precious stones on the way they cover. What are those precious stones? Those are unexplored relationships. In several cases people open accounts with a new bank while they already bank with other banks for a long time. These people, for a lot of reasons, don't operate the new accounts with full swing. The reason may range from not receiving the right response from the bank, finding the products not as viable as they thought etc. It may also be the fact that they open the account for a particular and limited purpose while the main accounts are operated in other banks where they have age old relationship and where they are Valuable customers. These customers, over a period of time, lose interest and the bonding is nipped in the bud. In effect, bank loses the opportunity of building connection with a prospective customer. Hence it is of paramount importance to check and verify the potential of each customer.

A scientific profile checking through personal rapport should bring to the light how potential is a customer, how strong is his / her relationship with other banks. With this information in hand all the newly acquired customers should be tapped I a planned move which should make them easy with the new family of the bank. They should be attracted with products and services and before much time is wasted, one more product should be added to the relationship over and above the basic account of the customers. Although for cheque and currency transactions the customers should ideally use the Alternate channels, it is desirable that there should be some amount of foot fall in the branch premises else the personal touch with the customers will be lost from the start. Once a new customer is bound by at least two products, the relationship can be run in auto-pilot mode and deepened provided the standard of Service does not fall. And here comes the Cross Sales.

Cross Sales plays a major role in the above. During the footfall of customers, the branch personnel should try to sell to the customers products other than what he has not bought so far. A general customer should be locked with minimum 2.50 products. The branch needs to identify what product a customer is not using and try to push the same. Since customers are flesh and blood, psychological approach is a way to sell. For instance, Jone's Syndrome is a characteristic where one comes into competition with friends, neighbour and relatives. *Mr. Haripada primarily shows reluctance in buying a car loan and his Personal Banker remarks - "Sir your next door neighbour possesses two cars. The latest was his present to his wife on their last anniversary". Haripada becomes soft and starts soft queries regarding the products. One day a new car is driven to his portico. Thus, without fresh acquisition of customers, a bank can and should increase the volume of business up-grading the existing individual customers.*

The conclusion is - Net-worth of a new customer is not known to the bank in the initial stage of relationship. The customer may be considerably potential or a high net-worth one. Hence there is no room for indifference to new customers and they should be attended from the beginning and hooked into relationship. This is always an opportunity and if this cannot be utilized, it will be a clear Loss of Opportunity which is a bad sign for any Retail bank. A story as under will help in understanding this.

It was 1994 when I was heading a major Retail branch of Standard Chartered Bank in a posh area in Kolkata. One afternoon an elderly couple came to my cabin. That day, for some reason, I was under the weather since morning. However, the couple sat before me and enquired about a fixed deposit of rupees fifty thousand with us. They actually were not able to remember if the same deposit was with us at all. I asked my Assistant Manager to take a look into the matter and was silent. After a while, the gentleman asked "May I have a cup of coffee? My lips are dried up" I came back to my senses and realized where I had gone wrong. Coffee was arranged for them. I started talking to them and during the course of discussion it came out that three years back he had sold his flat to one big singer in Mumbai and the proceeds of Rs.1 Crore was placed in RBI bond. This was due for maturity next month. I started deepening the relationship with the couple and in due course the same amount of rupees 1 crore was placed with Standard Chartered Bank. This is a lesson that a person should not be judged with what he maintains in a bank. He may be a highly potential customer in a competitor bank. Adequate process in Relationship Management can unearth such facts.

Moreover, it is an ongoing process of lifting a customer from one level to the next level of value relationship. We will discuss the Pyramid of Relationship or customer base when we enter the land of Priority Banking. Let us complete the last part of the exercise, which is Attrition.

REFERRALS

This area of acquisition is also very important and bank may derive a good amount of benefit out of this exercise. A customer, whether potential or non-potential may have valuable acquaintances and be well connected. Banks should explore such area exploit the hidden opportunity. Periodic Referral programs should involve all sorts of customers and referrals are to be acquired for regular drives to net those connections for future conversions into relationships. It is easy to approach existing customers who regularly transact with the bank and to get referrals from them of prospective individuals. A happy customer will be happy to help the bank in this especially when there are various prizes and recognitions are attached to such programs.

But before going for Attrition of unprofitable customers, the bank should explore their contacts as well. Even if a customer is not a profitable relationship as per the consideration of a bank or even if a customer is indifferent with his bank and maintains minimum relationship, he/she may also be acquainted with a high network person. These unprofitable customers, after identification, can be taken in Referral programs and contacts of potential individuals may be obtained to get them into relationships.

ATTRITION

This part of the exercise is Attrition or "Get rid of the unwanted". After acquiring a customer for the bank and taking him/her through the process of Retention, Deepening and then pushing him/her to the Up Gradation channel, the MIS will show a group of customers who are hard to get placed on the Profitability tray. They are the residual lot who might have opened basic accounts with certain purpose in mind but shortly decided not to be very active in operating their accounts for multiple reasons which may not be short lived but may be of low value base. It is seen that even after repeated effort to make these relationships viable, the efforts go in vain mainly due to the unwillingness of the customers or in many cases the customer being not so potential. In such cases bank needs to consider attrition of such customers in order to reduce cost of operation against these unprofitable customers. As it is, cost of transaction in an alternate channel is 20% of the cost of transaction due to a customer at branch premises. This attrition is also an ongoing process of identifying dry leaves and unwanted weeds and to steer clear the same periodically.

For any bank the above steps like Acquisition, Retention, Deepening, Up Gradation, Attrition and Referral are 'one after another' and also 'simultaneous' activities towards creating a strong base of Retail customers. Once this purpose is satisfactorily served, the bank should ready itself for the next very important part to set up Priority Banking facility or High Net-worth Cell for the high potential and top notch customers. This is a high sensitive zone, and needs a detailed understanding before entering through the main door.

To summarise, creating a strong, profitable and meaningful basic customer base, a bank needs to follow and execute a systematic process of Marketing, Sales and Services well supported by Centralized Operations which can be best explained by the picture as under:

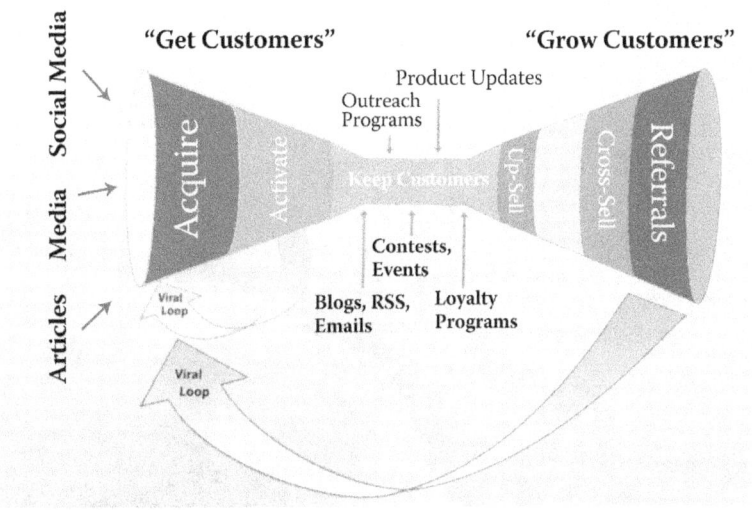

PRIORITY BANKING

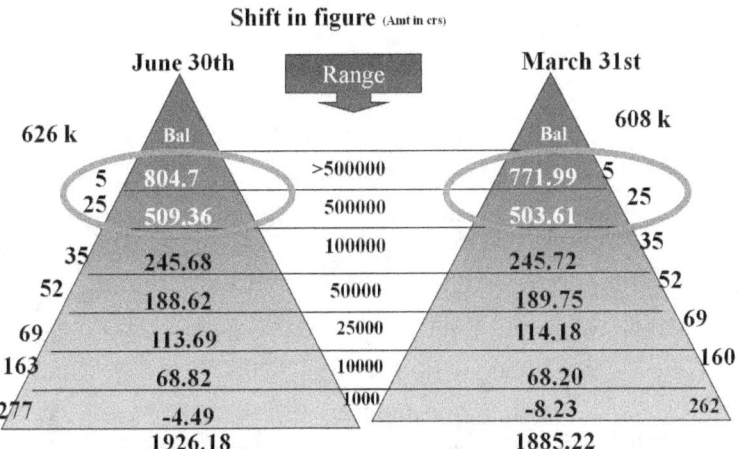

Less than 5% a/cs contribute to approx 70% of the Retail liability book

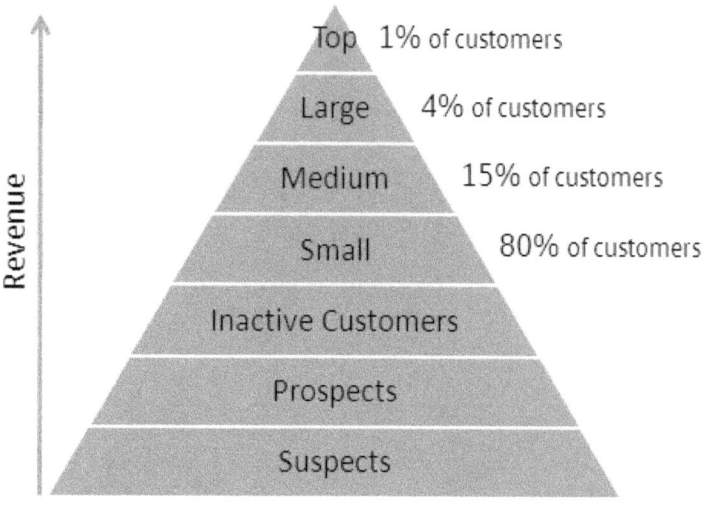

Pareto's Principle

We have passed through the gate of the most sensitive Customer area. Let's look at Pareto's Principle before we get introduced to the most delicate group of customers in any bank.

The observation made by Pareto is 80% of the effects. This principle of Pareto is very well applicable to business as well. In banking we see that 80% of the business comes from 20% of the customers whereas only 20% of the business is contributed by 80% of the customers.

Let us take a simple example to approach to this principle. If one makes an attempt to make a tasty fruit cake, she will surely put cashew nut, dried grapes, cherry and other fruits in the batter in a particular proportion and bake. If the blending is accurate and the baked hot cake is cut into several pieces, we will find that in every single piece of the cake the proportion of the ingredients are same. Likewise, when we analyse a customer book of any bank/branch, we find that 20% of the customers contribute to 80% of the business. Of late there is a further change in the concept. The revised principle says that it is not 20% but only 10% of the customers help a bank build 90% of the value in the book.

If we agree with the above, then a scary picture emerges. It clearly implies that if, for any reason, the 10% of those top end customers decide to severe the relationship, any bank will have to pull its shutter down!! It, then, comes to the highest priority level to ensure that these top notch customers are consistently happy with the bank. This does not mean, the rest 80% of the customers are to be neglected or to bid them good bye. Remember, the 80% makes the whole of 100% and if not explored there may be a good lot of customers who are high potential, are hiding themselves without using the bank fully. Hence mining in the 80% of the field is an ongoing process to identify these people and upgrade them gradually to the level of at least top 20%.

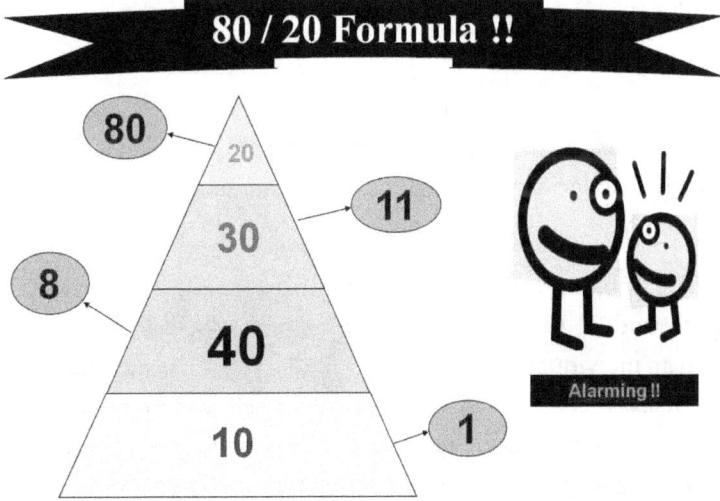

It's important to know this sensitive segment, to understand what they expect from bank or from their own life. Interestingly, this particular segment attracts us to Maslow's Hierarchy which we must discuss before understanding the top notch customers. Let us take a glance at the picture below:

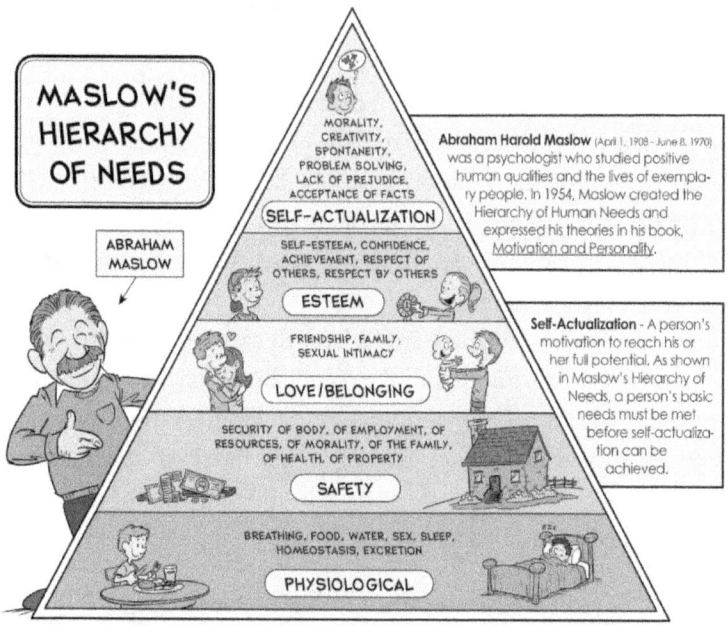

Although the above picture is self explanatory, let's give some thought over it. An individual, after birth on this planet, advances through certain stages which are essentially influenced by human psychology.

In the 1st phase, one is driven by the basic needs like food, water, oxygen and all that can be termed as physiological requirements. When an individual is elevated to the 2nd level, the needs change and are transformed into sense of Security which comes from Money, Insurance, Employment, Health. The need for Shelter is also there when one goes for house, flats and everything that are associated to Safety. Once these are fulfilled, the person feels the emotion related desires like Love, Affection, Family, Sexual intimacy etc. Upon graduation to the next level, an individual is psychologically massaged by self as well as by society when the requirements of the person are completely different and can be termed **"Self Esteem"**. Here one gains self confidence as he moves through his achievements and enjoys respects of others. These changes in mindset push the person to the last level which is generally known as **"Self Actualization"**. Here we find these people spiritually elevating themselves to a level where they find themselves above the small things like superstitions, jealousy, prejudices etc and instead they display traits like creativity, kindness, morality, problem solving and so on. Here we get a person with magnanimity of soul after he covers a long journey of his life through ups and downs, sunshine and storms.

Our focus is on these people who form a different segment altogether and they only constitute the top end of the customer pyramid. It's highly important to know the behavioural pattern of this segment – their expectations from the bank, social psychology, likes and dislikes etc. A close look of an analytical mind may reveal the following:

WE CALL THEM HIGH NETWORTH GROUP

And they are characterized by:

- Successful in life
- Ego and Elegance
- Eyes on Riches
- Awareness and Expectations

We can identify this segment at the last two levels of Maslow's pyramid of hierarchy. Let us look for them:

Firstly, they need Recognition in social and professional circles hence they go for Luxury homes, high model cars – chauffer driven. They enjoy membership of reputed Clubs spending time there socializing over drinks, on golf greens or billiard tables. They prefer to keep themselves physically fit by Swimming, playing Tennis, Badminton etc. Overall, they lead a happy go lucky life at a stage when Success has been achieved in life.

Secondly, we watch their Self Esteem when we see them gently advertising themselves with initials on their shirts, using special and costly cosmetics, smoking high branded cigars. This relates directly to their Egoistic mind which develops as they climb up the ladder. However, this, sometimes, help banks in selling products to them. We will discuss later.

In the Self Actualization phase we find them getting involved in Charities, Trusts, Memorials which earn them name when all other earthly desires are fulfilled.

Broadly the people on the top of Pareto's pyramid eye for the following:

- Recognition
- Exclusivity
- Value of time
- Return on Investment
- Liquidity
- Security
- Identity
- Name and Fame

A bank committed to Retail Banking need to deal with these customers carefully since they are the plinth of business. Let us see how to handle Priority customers, to retain them and also to derive maximum contribution from them:

RECOGNITION -

1. Know them personally.
2. Differentiate them from others.
3. Keep in constant touch both socially and officially.
4. Let them feel that they are valued as a class apart.

These customers develop **Zones' Syndrome** hence banks may tickle their sentiments to get more business. For example, Mr. Rao has a car and bank wants to sell a car loan to him who expresses his lack of interest. Now if he is reminded that his neighbour, Mr. Padmanabhan, has two and Mr. Rao should present one for his wife, there may be instant result and Mr. Rao will go for a car loan.

EXCLUSIVITY AND VALUE OF TIME -

"I am not a commoner. I am in a hurry and need seclusion".

1. Treat them in an exclusive area.
2. Help them do their Transactions in privacy.
3. There should be Pop up in screens so that they can be identified as Priority customers.
4. They are busy hence a quick disposal pleases them.

RETURN > LIQUIDITY > SECURITY

"My money should be secured, earn high and at the same time I need to get it back whenever I require."

1. Provide them good Advisory services.
2. Create confidence and build trust.
3. TRUST plays pivotal role here.

SELF ESTEEM > IDENTITY > ACTUALIZATION

1. Give presentations which massage their ego.
2. Call them on events and let them hoist flag, cut cakes or cut ribbons.
3. Make them hold chairs on occasions.
4. Periodic touches – personal or electronic.
5. Keep them happy with their banker.

At the end of all efforts, banks need to aim at locking each of their individual Priority Banking customers with minimum 3.50 products on an average. That is the thumb rule for this top end segment. If the top 20% customers are kept happy, half the job of any bank is done in securing current position and also in garnering more such high value relationships through their existing HN customers who are presumably well connected. They may help their banker by giving references and also by recommending the bank to their connections.

BUSINESS RUN RATE

The most important activity that peeps through the wind screen is Run Rate. When a bank sets its business book targets at the beginning of a year, it becomes the responsibility of the team to achieve these figures related to Assets or Liabilities. There should be uniformity in pace all through the year else cost for bank shoots up with related anxieties.

For instance, if the target for liability in a particular year is set at Rs.200 crores, the same should be divided among months keeping in mind the seasonal variations and other associated factors, financial or social. Again if the target is achieved much before the year end, it means either the market was underestimated or the team is on their over achievement. In that case the target may be revisited and reset. However, all through the year the run rate needs to be monitored segment by segment, product by product and also activity by activity.

For instance:

- For clean sweep from the market through Direct Sales team
- For fresh acquisition through referrals from existing customers
- For fresh acquisition from existing customers as In-branch sales
- Up-gradation of existing customers – both value and numbers
- Deepening of values from existing customers

It is easier to monitor performance and identify low or high performing areas if the total target is split among those above.

CUSTOMER SEGMENTATION

It's absolutely imperative to know our existing and prospective customers by segments. To me this segmentation is a bit queer. While an individual may be in Service holder segment and behaves in a particular pattern, the same person is a father or husband and will behave differently in a different role. However, the basic segmentation shows as under:

MINDSET   MAPPING

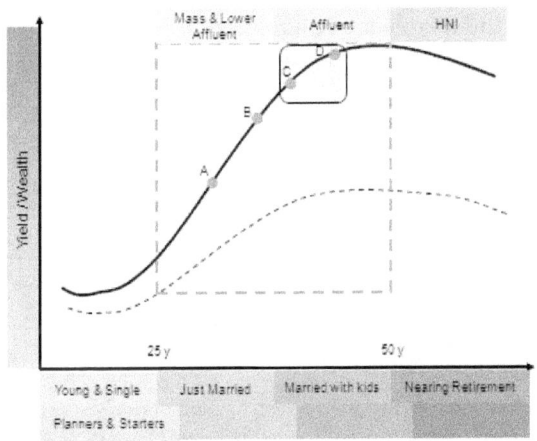

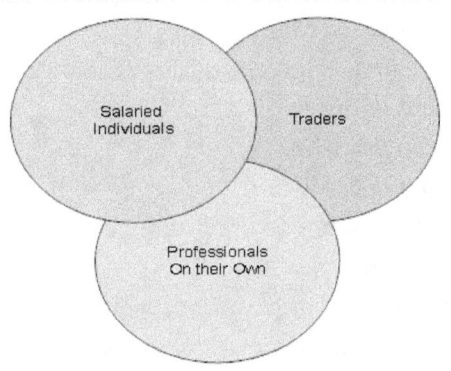

Salaried Individuals – type 1

Young, First time employees

- < 2 years experience
- New found disposable incomes
- High spends on entertainment (eating out, socializing)
- Quasi Brand conscious
- Demanding consumers in terms of the value they seek from all purchases
- Ambitious & driven
- Risk takers (not much to lose)
- Need independence & liquidity
- Modern outlook
- Optimistic – can change the world
- Start life successfully
- Banking needs – basic banking, debit / credit cards, personal loans

Salaried Individuals – Type 2

Young adults

- 6-8 years experience
- Limited budgets, high expense
- Regular spends (eating out, socializing & shopping)
- Acquiring assets (car, house, white goods)
- Looking into the future (savings)
- Expects a certain level of quality & service
- Ambitious & driven
- Calculated risk takers
- Independent & Modern
- Optimistic (starting to bring about a change)
- Success defined clearly
- Banking needs – basic banking, debit / credit cards, personal / auto loans, investments

Salaried Individuals – Type 3

Established & Constantly upgrading

- 15 years experience
- Spends more family centric(kids, shopping, holidays)
- Acquiring wealth (assets as well as investments)
- Discerning consumer – no compromises
- Rationalizes expenditure
- Ambitious, Driven, Dynamic
- Calculated risks
- Modern & Optimistic
- Attaining Success
- Banking needs – car / home loans, mutual funds, insurance, Investments

Salaried Individuals – Type 4

Multiple sources of income

- Well Established
- Seen as performers
- 15 years + experience
- Spends on hobbies, long distance travel, designer labels, networking
- Acquired wealth, enhancing it Living life today
- Commands Quality & Service (seen as birth right)
- Used to luxury, however believes he is a wise spender
- Hedonistic, Ambitious & Driven
- Can afford to take a few risks
- Modern & Optimistic
- Attained Success, redefining it
- Banking needs – full service, advisory services, Investments options

Start up Traders

- Start up mindset - Straddling between growing business and making profit
- Conservative spends (uses every rupee to enhance business)
- Spends primarily on asset building (security net)
- Ambitious, Dynamic, Driven
- Networking to create new opportunities
- High potential, 'can do' attitude
- Demanding consumer (extremely value driven)
- Independent minded
- Calculated risk taker
- Success defined, plans to reach it clear
- Banking needs – basic banking, business loans, investment options

Established Traders

- Transiting from entrepreneur to Industrialist
- Established in his business
- Wealth management & enhancement
- Used to quality, spends on enhancing lifestyle, however wise spender
- Straddle from being label conscious to down to earth simple living
- Ambitious, Dynamic, Driven, Visionaries
- 'Can do' attitude
- Leaders who set the path
- Discerning consumer
- Innovator
- Seasoned risk taker
- Attained Success, redefining it
- Banking needs – full service, advisory services, Investments options

CHANNEL MANAGEMENT

Retail banks work with multi pronged channels to attack the market picking up the relationships and nurturing those customers towards growth of the book. Let us see which are these channels which are integral part of a Retail Bank:

- ➤ Branch Banking team which includes Operations Manager
- ➤ Relationship Managers or Affluent Market team
- ➤ Direct Sales Team of Feet on Street
- ➤ Business Development Team

All the above channels need to work in tandem with a selfless mind and weave the network of Business. All the channels should operate in the following discipline:

A bank operates in the market primarily with its Branch platform and then goes for new acquisition through Direct Sales. Up gradation of a customer or a group of customers rests on Priority Banking or Preferred Banking team while servicing the whole lot of customers outside the branch premises is done by all available alternate banking channels. Now, it is important for all the four teams to distribute among themselves

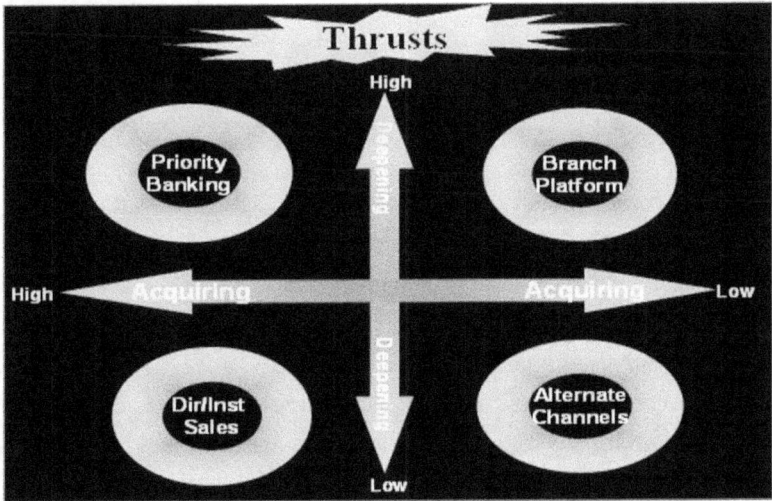

the responsibility of Acquisition and deepening with required thrusts. Somewhere the thrust on acquisition is higher whereas in some cases the thrust of deepening the relationship is higher and vice –versa. The diagram below should best explain the roles.

It is of paramount importance that all the channels should come under ONE UMBRELLA from where the direction should be from one head. Failing which there will be conflict of interest leading to chaos defeating the sole purpose of doing business. The following picture reveals how the personnel of various channels work in an overlapping scenario where each one is to become a perfect team member and is ready to shoulder responsibility in other areas of operation.

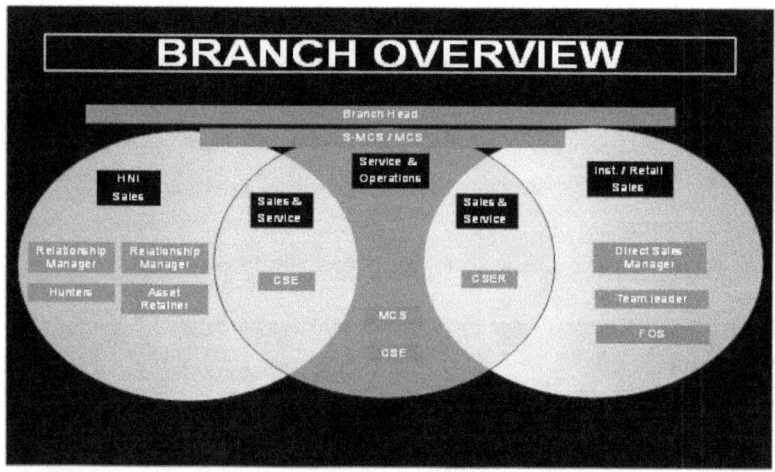

Unless members of all the channels work in a harmony, the desired result will remain a far cry. Activities are overlapped, purpose is one and team must be ONE.

RESPONSIBILITIES

Time has come to discuss accountability or responsibilities pertaining to various positions. As I say, Retail Banking is an integrated team where high commitment to individual responsibilities leads to the group success. Let us discuss the general structure of a Retail team in a big branch.

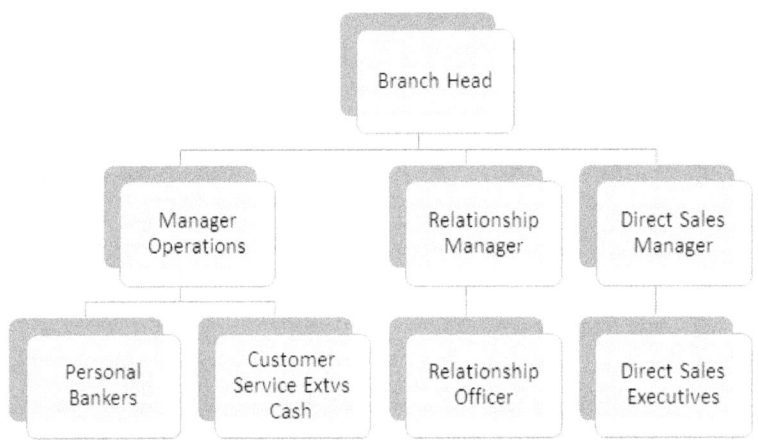

Let us take from the Top:

BRANCH HEAD

Branch Head of a branch is the Chief Executive Office (CEO) of the office with overall responsibility to run the Retail business with his team. He is to ensure that:

o   The growth of number of customers is as per projection of the branch. In this job, the Direct Sales team under the related manager do their job.

o   The branch builds a strong deposit book by selling the Liability products to the customers.

o   He creates a profitable Asset portfolio for the branch to generate a steady income. In this job the Branch Head also needs to ensure that no asset relationship goes bad and becomes unprofitable.

o   A required thrust is given to sell the third party products to strengthen the bottom line of the balance sheet by earning sufficient Fee income. As CEO of the branch he should also be on the vigil so that no wrong selling is done and customer feels cheated.

o The Branch Head needs to socialize enough in the command area so that he creates an image for both the bank and himself. He can use his market intelligence to feel the pulse of the area and chalk out business strategy accordingly.

o A Branch Head is also the Human Resource head in his own area and needs to run his team as per HR policy of the bank. The business depends how he nurtures his team and deals with individual members taking care of their wishes and aspirations.

o To be a successful Branch Head in business, there must be a motivated team working under him. He should imbibe a sense of belongingness, an aggression which helps any force in the market to achieve the mission.

o A morning huddle is a modern day prescription for any Branch Head who should make it a routine for the branch. In this exercise, every day before the branch starts its daily operations, all the employees must gather for 10-15 minutes where they discuss the important achievements/challenges the previous day. The team also discusses their plans for the day and any other crucial matter to be looked at.

o As an individual, a Branch Head should be able to maintain an ideal and appreciable relationship across all levels – his juniors or superiors.

o End of it, the Balance sheet of the branch matters. The bottom line needs to be in bold blue with no leakage of income in any way.

o Last of all, the Branch head needs to give adequate respect and importance to other verticals of business to give and take the benefit of the franchisee.

The following picture gives a synopsis of responsibilities of a Branch Head in his/her place:

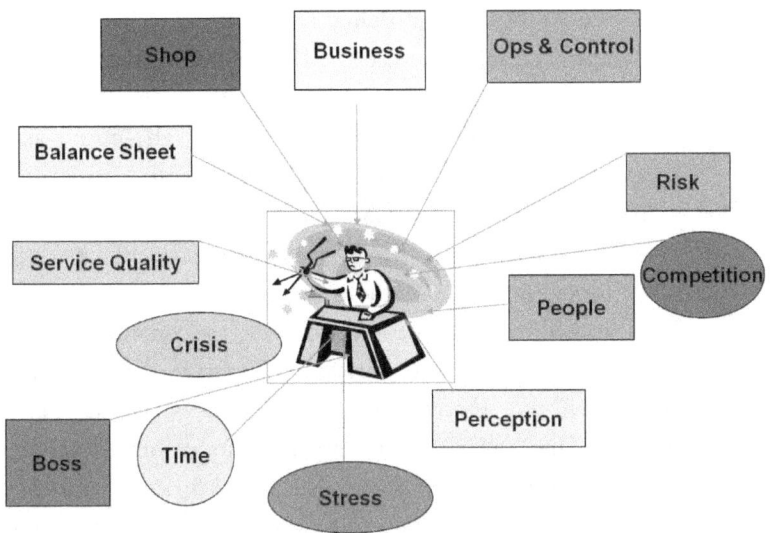

MANAGER OPERATIONS

The most important person, next to Branch Head, is Manager Operations (MOP) who is, by all sense, is the office master of the unit. This role is very important being the custodian and watchman of the unit. He/she is the eyes and ears of the branch. Let us examine what are the responsibilities attached to this role:

o Operations Manager is the person who should be in total control of the day to day proceedings from start of the day (SOD) to the end of it (EOD).

o The areas that broadly come under Manager Operations are Cash, ATM, Clearing, Collections, Account opening formalities, Safe Keeping of records and documents, Locker related accountability, Book keeping, Premises maintenance etc.

o The Cash Officers under MOP have to ensure flawless accounting of both payments and receipts over the counter and to close the cash book at EOD tallying the currencies. Cash in the ATM should also be accounted and at EOD all currencies are to be kept back in the chest under the signature and supervision of MOP who should be rigid in his supervision.

o In single window system cheques for local collections are also deposited with the Cash Officers who account for all the cheques deposited and place with clearing house. Debit Notes are often generated out of clearing transactions and the MOP needs to ensure that both Debit Note payable and receivable books are as clean as possible.

o The Personal Bankers' primary duty is to sell and cross sell all products available in the racks. However, they need to ascertain that all the Account Opening Documents (AOD) are obtained from the customers strictly as per norms adhering to the "Know Your Customer" or KYC guidelines. And as Manager Operations, it is his responsibility to check and verify that each AOD fulfils the laid down norms. On satisfaction, the AODs are to be sent to Central Processing Unit for opening the accounts.

o To maintain a high quality of service on the floor comes under the accountability of MOP and he stands by ideal Turn-Around-Time (TAT) and over the desk delivery of services flawlessly.

o Cross Sales is essentially the stretch objective of MOP who sees to it that customers garnered by the Direct Sales Team are not only retained with good services but also additional products are sold. A general customer is expected to be locked with more than two products and thus the relationship with the individual is deepened over a period of time.

o Over and above, the Manager Operations drives a team comprising of Cash Officers and Personal Bankers. It is expected that he nurtures the team with his Leadership quality and takes the best out of the team. Additionally, there are business officials like Relationship Manager and Manager Direct Sales who MOP needs to work with in tandem helping them developing business. More often than not, conflicts arise with respect to observing rules and regulations. MOP needs to manage these conflicts. Branch Head may be involved in this if required.

o End of everything, MOP is the guard in chief for all regulatory and compliance issues in the branch. It is his/her responsibility to ensure that the branch is Audit compliant and obtains more than "Satisfactory" remark for the Audit teams, Internal or statutory.

RELATIONSHIP MANAGER

The position of Relationship Manager has gone through evolution since the eighties. During the eighties whenever a branch of a bank used to be opened, a senior or retired person was posted to the branch for some period to meet people in the locality and to bring awareness of the bank informing them of the advent of the bank in the command area. After some time, once the branch gets settled, this person generally used to leave the location. In the next phase, in the nineties, this same person appears as Marketing officer to penetrate in the adjoining areas where the bank operates. This Marketing officer was generally a young person working as a hand of the Branch Head. Presently we see Relationship Manager in the Retail branches handling the high Net-worth relationships of the branch and garner new potential customers for the branch. Relationship Manager (RM) is essentially the business wing of the branch where he is expected to :

Do micro-market analysis of the command area of his branch and a full profile of the area should be in his finger tips.

He should know his high potential customers deeply and establish a personal relationship so as to build in them a confidence in him.

RM needs to do data mining on an ongoing basis and identify those customers in the branch who do not maintain high balance but are immensely potential and may be banking with other banks where he even is a high net-worth customer.

RM is given targets both in numbers and value. Only value driven targets get lost in numbers hence the branch should grow both vertically and horizontally in respect of building a HNI book.

Overall, a Relationship Manager is responsible for acquisition of new customers from High Net-worth segment and also to upgrade the existing customers from level to level in value so that over a period of time the aggregate value of Affluent Market book is increased to the benefit of the branch.

Socializing is what a RM should do on an ongoing basis. He should create confidence of the customers in him by keeping continuous touch with his customers. This helps him in mining more business from this segment and thus enriching his portfolio. If we follow the behavioural pattern of the Affluent segment, this group of people frequently socialize in their high end circle and do expect to be recognized by their banks as Priority customers. Thus banks often organize parties for their Privileged customers who appreciate this gesture from their bankers. However, it is for the Relationship Managers to utilize such platform to get mixed with their customers and deepen the relationship as business practice.

At the same time Relationship Manager should never compromise with the Quality of acquisition. This position is responsible for scanning those customers whom he is inviting to the branch.

As regards account opening documentation, since value of relationship is on the higher side, a RM should co-operate with MOP to make the file flawless to avoid any future regulatory complication.

DIRECT SALES MANAGER

Starting from the inception of a branch Direct Sales Manager (DSM) shoulders the key responsibility to drive his Sales Executives in the command markets and pick up relationships to help the branch roll the business. What all are expected of a DSM are as under :

1. To build up a formidable sales team through ongoing training and motivation.
2. To build up a clear idea about the nature of the command area profile as per Pico Market analysis done for the purpose.
3. To develop a picture of the competition and major business / individual potential customers in and around the area.
4. To bombard the area with leaflets and personal representations bringing awareness of the bank among the residents.
5. To conduct local campaigns with canopies and umbrellas and make people understand the features and benefits of the products.

Even after the branch is opened and starts operating, the Direct Sales Executives must keep regular touch with their acquired relationships for quite some time till the new customers get accustomed to the environments and services of the bank.

Every individual member of the Direct Sales team must ensure that quality of acquisition is not compromised in any way and there is no deviation from the standard norms in respect of Account Opening formalities. We have come a long way from what was there decades back and presently every individual members must be vigilant about perfectness in documentation else there may be trouble in future days.

APEX RETAIL TEAM

Let us now travel upward to see understand how a Retail Bank operates at its macro level. For any Retail bank there is always a Human Structure as below where the top two lines comprise Strategy desk which decides which way the Retail business will move :

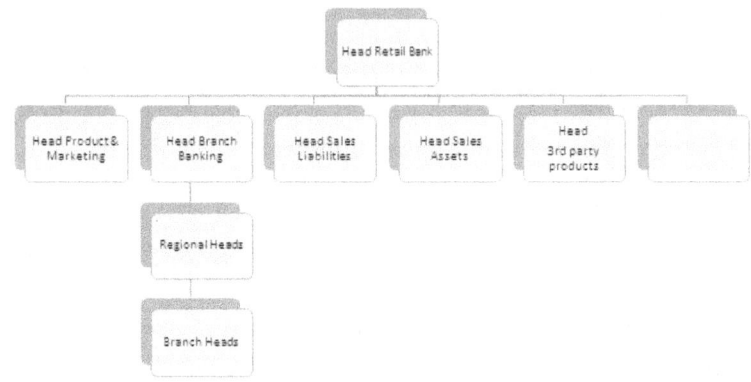

The Apex structure above of a Retail bank is the core team to decide the direction of the Retail business vertical and also the strategy for the same. Let us visit their conference rooms and see what all happens there, what are the Dos and Don'ts for the Central Retail Management :

FINANCIAL PLANNING

At the beginning of financial year the team sit with the Bank's aggregate target on the board and create the projected balance sheet which will incorporate the targets for Liabilities, Assets, 3rd Party products which together boil down to both Interest income and Fee income contributing to the bottom line of the balance sheet. In this exercise all other expenses including HR cost which occupy the major pie.

Ideally these targets are distributed in four quarters month by month for monitoring of the progress of business. The Retail Head and his team sits with the Regional Heads to allocate their shares of targets which the Regional Heads in turn distribute among the branches under their control in the same manner. Thus the total Financial projection of a Retail vertical is made to start a year.

CAPACITY PLANNING

Next in line comes Capacity Planning which is utterly important to achieve the business volumes. With the increase of Business volume there is a capacity gap in respect of Human Resource, Branch or ATM network and related administrative needs. All these are to be taken into account to build a budget and these additional capacities are to be incorporated in budget in financial value.

BUSINESS STRATEGIES

Business strategies are multi pronged. The core Retail team chalks out the strategies from time to time. It deals with (a) Product Design and Product performance (b) Network expansion and management (c) Human Resource induction and allocation (d) Blue Ocean strategy and so on. Let us take few of these for short discussion.

PRODUCT DESIGN & PROMOTION

In order to penetrate into the market, and to combat with competition Retail team need to design new products from time to time depending upon the demand of customers and nature of products offered by competitor banks. The central Marketing team do it in consultation with the team. These products sometimes are launched in a limited geography, called Launch Pad for testing the reaction of the market. Later, on satisfaction of primary responses, the same product is spread across the country of select regions. Sales wings at the branch level are the conveyor belts for the products in the market. Hence a close co-ordination between the Sales and Marketing wings brings success for a product.

Since customers do not switch their loyalties to a bank simply for a mere difference in rate, for promotion of a newly launched product advertisements in bill boards and news papers should not continue for a long period of time. It may attract unnecessary cost. Hence advertisements of a product should be planned for a limited period.

It should be to bring awareness and to use as a Teaser. However, it does not end with a product promotion but continuous monitoring of the performance of a product is necessary. If it is found that a particular product is not taken in the market as per expectation of the bank, it is wise to withdraw the product to avoid costs of marketing and sales.

PRODUCTS – Mass /Mass Affluent Market

The core Retail brigade does also adopt plans to penetrate into mass and mass affluent market in the areas they make in road. And Sales team is not enough unless the team is supported by right products – need based products with right features and benefits. To arrest the mass market, a product acceptable and attractive to general population is needed. In 1997 HDFC Bank had launched "FREEDOM ACCOUNT" with no minimum balance required. It was a novel product and a big success in the markets enabling HDFC Bank garner thousands of accounts across the country. Although later a big number of relationships were found un-remunerative, the bank was immensely benefitted with huge number of good and potential account holders by deepening the relationships where the total value went up to enviable heights. These huge number of account holders helped the bank build a valuable book not only with all sorts of products but also by referring new relationships which were finally brought from other banks too. This was replicated much later in 2001 by Bank of Punjab and in 2006 by DCB launching "SWAGAT" and "FREE STYLE" accounts respectively with required modifications and adding new features and benefits. These two basic Savings Bank products too found immense success in the regions where the thrusts were given by the two banks.

The strategy is to garner as many Savings Accounts in the bag as possible and then gradually develop the relationship over a period of time by personal touch and cross selling other products to them so that the relationship value goes up with multi products be these Liability, Asset or Third Party . the aim should be to (1) to lower the cost of fund (2) Increase Interest income and (3) hike up Fee income periodically with through a strong book of Relationship.

To sum up :

- Products, Assets or Liability, are to be developed keeping in mind the need of the customers, of target segments.
- Starting from conceptualization to development of a product the bank should keep in mind geography, society, economy and other associated factors.
- It is wise to identify a launch pad to test the product instead of launching the same across the soil of the country.
- In the semi-final stage, feedback should be taken from Sales personnel, outbound or in-branch.
- The bank needs to respect the product and engage the spirit of employees passionately.
- The employees need to believe in the product and should be in a mind to buy it else there may be reasons to worry.
- Periodical monitoring of sales vis-à-vis target should be done to assess the effectiveness of the same in the market.
- While designing products, the profitability of the product should be kept at the back of mind. Sometimes free bees added to the products and eventually the free bees eat away the profitability of the product. Although often, to combat with competition, free bees are needed but care should be taken that there is no erosion in profit.
- The following picture, I think, will best explain what happens if a product is developed without understanding the nature of need by the customer and if there is no co-ordination among various departments.

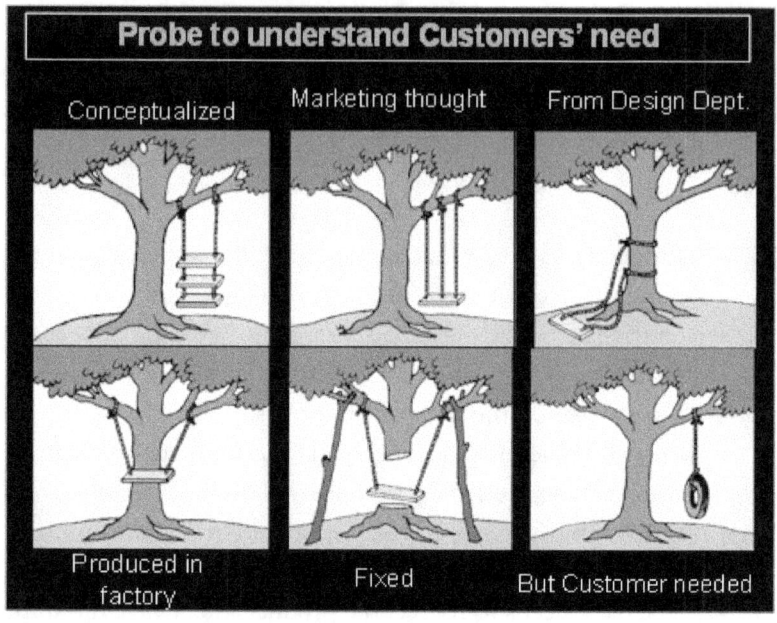

CUSTOMER PROFITABILITY

Starting from Product development through Marketing, Sales, Acquisition, Deepening to Up Gradation, whatever is done, the ultimate purpose is to arrive at customer profitability which ultimately leads to the profitability of the Retail vertical. The aim should be to convert every individual customer a profitable relationship and for that purpose, a right combination or mix of products is to be sold to a customer. There should be provision for appropriate MIS to periodically ascertain if a customer is profitable to the bank and accordingly plan for the individual may be adopted. If, after repeated efforts, a customer does not turn out to be a profitable relationship for the bank then attrition is The Way. However, it may be examined whether the individual contributes to a segment or group profitability.

NETWORK EXPANSION & MANAGEMENT

Organic or inorganic, growth in network is important during the business journey for any Retail bank and this is to be done adroitly. Core Retail team takes this decision and adopts strategy for the same. The team identifies various potential pockets, conducts survey, assess strengths and opportunities in view of presence of competition and then decides on opening the branch. The same applies in the case of installation of ATMs. A branch should ideally be supported by ATMs in the peripheral areas where footfall is sufficient enough to sustain cost of running an ATM. While taking decision on network expansion, a bank must examine that in a certain pocket the competition does not get cluttered with entry of presence of too many competitors. Unless the bank's brand image is pretty strong in the market, banks should be careful about it else the expected result may not be seen. Although banks have got their respective strengths, the market size may go against a bank in respect of garnering relationships.

This is being noticed very recently when a number of Small Finance Banks have entered the market followed by IDFC and Bandhan Bank. Although RBI expects these Small finance Banks to help in Financial Inclusion by penetrating into lower income bracket of population but since these banks are opening quite a considerable number of branches in the urban areas and are all out to pick up deposits from people with higher interest rates, this may lead to cluttered competition building pressure on other banks too.

NETWORKING & BUSINESS

Networking and Retail business are interconnected and it needs market intelligence to be effective in this area. Let us take up a case as under :

To lower cost of fund, a bank needs to emphasize on CASA acquisition and ideally CASA should be around 50% of the total deposit if not a bit more. Now, for acquisition of Current account which is zero cost for a bank a localised operations or servicing don't really work since any trade is linked to various locations of the country and business account is an inter city matter where payments and receipts are made majorly across industrial locations where productions are made and cities where the produces are traded. Hence a Retail bank must consider presence in those locations or cities. The following locations are to be connected to woo Business accounts and to serve them well :

> Ludhiana and Delhi (Karol Bagh) in North
> Mumbai (Kalba Devi), Ahmedabad and Surat in West
> Bangalore (Chikpet)
> Tamil Nadu (Koimbatore)
> Hyderabad (Abids)
> Kerala (Kochi)
> Kolkata (Burra Bazar) and Siliguri in East
> Guahati (Dispur) and Gangtok in North East

The above is just an example of how the business cities are to be connected so that the business organizations are at ease to deal with other business units at other locations using "At Par Cheques", RTGS, NEFT, Phone Banking and all. This trans state presence is of utmost business banking necessity.

BLUE OCEAN STRATEGY In Retail Banking

The core Retail team in any bank cannot keep aside Blue Ocean Strategy when deciding course of their business. Blue Ocean Strategy is (a) Opening up new uncontested Business opportunities (b) Creating new market for business (c) Making competition irrelevant.

Bank should be on its toes to search for hinterland where the team should step in with its arms and ammunition to capture the market before competition steps in and make the maximum in minimum possible time.

Juxtaposed to Blue Ocean Strategy is **Red Ocean Strategy** which not only cannot be ignored but also to be taken up before adopting the Blue Ocean. Red Ocean Strategy is (a) Mining the existing market and extract the full opportunity (b) Beating the competition in existing market and enhancing the strength with brand value (c) Exploiting the existing demand.

Overall, the above strategies are to be dealt and addressed simultaneously where a Retail Bank needs to develop on what is there already and to create what is not there with them. The core Retail Team, with its people across network, should be vigilant that new opportunities follow existing opportunities, existing strength is increased to take up new markets and to take on competition making them inferior in market.

Asset Liability Management

In every bank there is an Asset Liability Management (ALM) committee where the there will be a representative of the core Retail team. Normally Head Retail or Head Branch Banking attends this committee where the Asset – Liability position is assessed and accordingly decisions are taken on Interest Rates offered or charged and also investment decision is made. This is a very important body on which profitability of the bank or tackling competition in the market majorly depends.

Branch to Bank Profitability

Some small or start up banks often suffer from Profitability headache. I joined a bank in mid of first decade of this century and found that the bank was in loss. The Retail Head had no clue how to come out of the red figure. I found that many of the branches were in loss and the Retail Head was at a loss. However, the new Managing Director who had pulled me to the bank increased asset book aggressively and gradually the loss making branches was turned to profit one by one.

But the purpose of writing this section is to assert how important is Asset in Retail Banking. The same Managing Director had set a rule that when a new branch would be opened people would not wait for the Liability book to grow and then sell asset. He directed that the new branches would start operation with a good asset book so that from beginning itself the branch is in profit. Hence the responsibility of the Retail Asset team was to garner Loan accounts and set the Asset business rolling before the Liability book is born. It gave result and no new branch was showing Red figure in their bottom line irrespective of when it started its operations.

Risk Management

When a team runs a business it goes without saying that the same team does not fail to manage the risk of business. The most important part of Retail Bank is selling Assets in various forms of Retail Loans. Products are evolved for various segments of customers, Out bound Sales forces are engaged in the market, Branch Sales teams are motivated. All these are done to build a voluminous Retail Asset book for the bank with distributed risk and higher return. But the short history of Retail Bank in India has showed number of times and in number of banks that due to sheer lack of market intelligence, for over aggression in sales and for product in wrong time banks have suffered massive set back. People have seen how for certain banks huge number of Personal Loans and Credit Card exposure which are essentially unsecured loans, have gone bad. Market had witnessed how Car loans have been launched in wrong centres without doing necessary market research and credit behaviour appraisal. There are witnesses of banks being aggressively exposed in Housing Loan area followed by massive property devaluations thus ending up with limited sales.

All the above have happened on this soil and the responsibility goes to Risk Management and Asset team. Such probability, even after tastes of sour, has not been eliminated. Hence the Retail

Management teams need to be firm and rigid in managing risk of Assets. And better it is to manage it in pre-disbursal stage rather than crying post exposure.

Frauds – Proactive Measures

The term Risk is closely associated with another word, "Fraud". Retail Banking is huge in its day to day operations and is spread without limitation of boundary. It involves People, Cash, Cheques and Technology. If we look at the history of frauds committed, we will be surprised with its variety in nature, style, amount and more particularly type of people involved. Fraud may be committed by people within the bank, by customers of the bank or other bank and also by a non-employee or non-customer.

Fraud may be committed by exploiting trust, over confidence, using modern technology and so on. It is not always easy to pre-empt a fraud, to ensure that it does not happen because in that case there would not have been any fraud in banking. But Preventive measures can be and must be taken. What all can be such measures ?

a) Trust none but the set procedures.
b) Alertness is the key mantra.
c) Adequate knowledge in technology and Banking regulations/ operations
d) Strict adherence to operation manual
e) Zero compromise with ethics and values.

Years back we had interviewed a lady, Dipasree Ganguly for a managerial position in Operations. When asked what she was particular about, she replied "I don't want to do anything or get involved in anything in work place that steals away my sleep". I was highly moved with her response and do still remember her words.

Again, too much of trust in colleagues may be fatal. One instance may be apt in this case :

In a Retail branch of a new generation bank the branch manager was an efficient person with a sharp intellect. He impressed his superior to recruit a person as his Assistant Manager to look after operations so that he could concentrate in business related activities. So it was agreed by the superior. This Operations guy was solely in charge of Cash and his daily duty was to count and close the cash after the cashier closes the book. He was also supposed to accompany the cashier to the cash vault and ensure that all cash is kept in the safe. Following this he needed to sign the cash register in the evening.

While this was going smoothly for some period, this Ops in-charge became lazy and started depending upon the cashier to complete the closing formalities. Accordingly every day, after closing the cash and taking it to vault (for which the Ops guy used to part with his vault keys in high trust) and used to get the register signed. Finally, one day it was found that there was a shortage of cash to the tune of rupees fifty lacs. What actually happened, the cashier, finding the loose checks and balances by his boss, started shifting Rs.20000/- every day. Over a month, Rs.5000000/- was stolen. It came to light on the day the branch thought of transferring the accumulated cash to other bank. Here trust was the Hamartia that caused the fatal flaw.

Recently we come across a line of ATM related frauds where outside hands as a gang are also involved. Forgery in cheques is a commonly known fraud where customer or beneficiary of the amount is found to be involved, for example, alteration in cheque amount of change in the name of the beneficiary. Sometimes we come across frauds committed as a result of connivance between bank executives and customers / non-customers.

For all the above discussed types of fraud, strict vigilance from top to bottom is needed. It is of high importance to ensure that bank's operation manual is strictly adhered without any compromise. In this respect, sporadic audit by audit cell as well by vigilance is required.

Target Setting and Allocations

This area is directly linked with Business Direction of any organization. Any bank has the prime business objective to keep its share holders smiling hence at the of the financial year the share holders of the bank get expected return on their investment thus their confidence in the top management goes up. The Top management of a bank thus decides on the projected profit for a particular financial year and allocate the same to all the business verticals who, in turn, chalk out their top lines of business which should boil down to targeted profit. Eventually, a Retail Segment distribute the same business projections among the business heads, regions, clusters and branches. Plans are made and strategies adopted as per the projections.

In no or rare case, this target exercise is bottom up. It is always top down. Of course it is natural that target will flow according to the expectations of share holders and Top Management. But it is always wise to get the lower lines involved in budget exercise from the beginning otherwise it becomes a one sided game and targets often become unrealistic. In the case of imposing unrealistic targets up on the bottom lines of management, the results may be as under :

- If people in the market feel that the budget is pretty touch and unachievable, then after trying for some time they are engulfed with despair and finally frustration.
- If they find the target very easy to achieve, they will have a tendency to go slow which ends up with loss of real opportunities.
- If a unit finds out that target given to them is not justified in comparison to what has been allocated to their peer branch of same size and capacity, then dissatisfaction grows.

In view of the above a practical budget is always a result of proper understanding of market reality, people's behaviour, seasonal fluctuations, skills available within the system e.t.c and all these information are to be collected from people on the front and not from ivory towers. Often we find two types of targets. One is what is given to the force and the other is the softer one that top management keep it in their sleeves which are unfolded in Right time. Not a bad strategy, but this needs to be handled carefully.

While in the case of Corporate Banking or Investment banking the budget exercise is comparatively easy, when it it comes to Retail Banking vertical, it is complicated, laborious and time consuming. The reason is, in Retail banking there is involvement of a big number of human resource, sub-verticals and branches. Hence, for a core Retail team a systematic and calendarized approach is necessary well before the close of previous financial year.

Think Global, Act Local

What do we take form the above ? Unlike Corporate Bank, or Investment Banking vertical, Retail arena has its own nature where huge number of people, customers and and wide spread geography is involved and these are very typical of the soil of the country. Hence while adopting business strategy, setting targets (both for the vertical and individuals), rewriting planning or revisiting products, the Retail Bank management may bring reference of what all happen in foreign soil but their eyes need to be on the ground of the country. Equating nature of customers in the globe with those in our country may lead to devastation. I would like to bring an example to illustrate the above.

One highly successful and dynamic banking personality in Indian banking industry came to India and joined a bank as Managing Director to revive the bank which was dying in the hands of his predecessors. He came with a highly commendable record in his previous banks in Middle East and Europe where he had turned around few banks. To describe his personality, he was a cannon ball with a passion to perform always. A great Leader, this vibrant MD made his team ready and started the ball rolling. Within a year the picture looked bright and the second year was a jubilant one. With full energy he exerted pressure on his Asset team to triple their performance in least possible time.

Here was the mistake. During his long absence from his own country, he might have lost touch with the nature of the soil and misjudged with credit behaviour of Indians in mass and mass affluent market. Moreover, he had recruited a wrong person from wrong industry as Head of Retail Bank. Although eventually he was disillusioned with the Head Retail and bade him farewell, it was too late and a huge amount of retail loans went bad. A very sad story of a brilliant Retail Banker, but it was due to his not acting according to the reality of the market. He possibly had, in his mind, the good and honest market of the countries had worked.

MIS and Management

Day by day MIS has become an integral part of any management team and it can assertively be told about Retail Banks where, not only the core management team but also the layers down the line are extensively using MIS as a guiding tool which are used for decision making as well as taking corrective measures.

An MIS throws light on the movement of the graph of business, northward or downward. It tells the story of customer behaviour, their likes and dislikes. MIS talks of the bottom line trend at various periodicities e.t.c and e.t.c. Core Retail Management needs to make the full utilization of such MIS to use in business. Not only this, the MIS team should be always on their toes to develop on what the existing System is providing.

Human Resource Induction and Allocation

It's an important area where the Retail team decides induction of people to cope up with projected growth of the vertical and expansion of network. Here comes the question of major cost hence the induction may be in phased manner. Cost allocation may be rank wise and how much will be spent for which level of people is a decision that is made by the team.

Hiring from competition often becomes costly although a trained and experienced person is available in this process. But it is also cost effective to hire fresh blood and train them up. In this process a loyal group of people may be groomed up though it may seem a bit time consuming. We will discuss this more in relevant chapter as we move.

Compliance

Compliance is an area which is an inseparable part of accountability of any Bank hence core Retail team. In the course of business and especially in chasing various business targets business managers are sometime allured to take forbidden routes thus becoming over aggressive in acquisition. This tendency leads to violation of the path of rules. One instance may be cited.

A single branch bank in Bangalore once hired an apparently dynamic manager to drive their retail business. One day he met an Arab Sheikh in the course of business. The Sheikh visited the bank expressing his interest in short term deposit with highest interest rate available. The Sheikh was a foreigner visiting India for six months and that time maximum Fixed Deposit rate available was in NRNR (Non Resident Non Repatriable) which this manager sold to the foreigner expecting that this gentleman would not take back his fund before he leaves for Middle East. Unfortunately for him and also for the bank, this Sheikh faced urgency of fund within a fortnight and came back to the bank to withdraw his deposit. The CEO who was not aware of what wrong selling was done faced height of embarrassments for regulatory violation and had to literally beg to local RBI for a bail out. Fortunately, due to his good reputation in the market he could come out of the fiasco.

The Core Retail Management under the Corporate body of the bank must ensure that in the course of their doing business a smooth and mutually beneficial relationship is maintained with other verticals namely, Corporate Banking and Investment Banking. This is important to ensure that no business opportunity from outside is lost due to sheer inter-vertical rivalry. A business opportunity for Retail Bank may be used by other verticals as well and vice versa. End of it it's the interest of the bank as a whole for which all the vertical should work in tandem. The purpose of writing this paragraph is the observation of such unhealthy existence of different business columns in a bank.

This is seen mainly in modern banks where the organization structure is Profit centre wise and not the Pyramid structure like in PSU banks.

MICRO FINANCE – A DIFFERENT WORLD

While discussing various areas of Retail Banking, we have so far travelled through the upper side of the customer pyramid and connected Retail Banking with their life style only. But we have kept a big area aside and not taken into account the life of those people, their need, their dream and their way of living. It is the lower part of the pyramid in India which is populated by about 30 million people. These people live their lives Below Poverty Line which we call BPL in short. This huge population do not have access to the so called big banks simply because they don't have money hence not wanted by the banks.

As per latest yard stick, people with less than Rs.27,000/- annual income or below the daily purchasing power of USD.1.25 are marked below poverty line. To banks this segment is a burden and unprofitable hence hardly they get opportunity to do normal banking. Banks don't even extend any loan facility to them. While banks cannot be blamed for their indifference to BPL segment for lack of infrastructure, machineries and penetration, it is the hard reality that the BPL customers are neglected on their own soil.

Under the above condition, we found the wake of a number of Micro finance companies in the country during the first half of the first decade of the century. They rapidly spread their wings and penetrated both in urban and rural sectors increasing their asset books phenomenally. What initially was looking good, became pale with the start of the following decade and market underwent a massive pandemonium for the following reasons :

Absence of Regulatory control
Political intervention
Lack of wise leadership
In fight in Management
Greed and inefficiency
Lack of previous experience.

All the above factors led the new industry to an avalanche during early part of 2011 and the chaos had affected a major chunk of the Micro Finance companies in the country. However, with Reserve Bank stepping into the area and new regulations were formed, gradually the velocity of the storm calmed down and life became normal with business. But what is this business ? It is primarily Asset business lending to the people lying on the bottom most line. MFIs give loans in small tickets to groups and individuals for various business and personal purposes. The interest rates were as high as 30% however, with the new regulations and strictures being imposed, there are some controls there. Although default rates often shoots up in various places for various reasons like bad days in business, flood e.t.c the high returns cover up the losses and collection cost.

Since Micro Finance business needs high penetration into rural, semi-urban and even urban fields, it needs people too to carry out the exercise. In this process on one hand regulatory imposition restricting high rate of interest and on the other hand management cost was bringing the spread of earning down especially when such business houses were suffering from lack of low cost of fund.

In the second stage of development when it was found that all these MFIs were suffering from fund crises since they are not allowed to take deposits from the public, RBI allowed ten of such companies to float Small Finance Banks who can not only lend to the lower end of the population but can lift deposits from public. Ujjivan, Equitus, Jan Finance are few names who emerged in this field showing a good governance and adroit business policies. This will enable them to have access to low cost fund and increase the spread of earning. A couple of years before this happened when, Bandhan, the leading Micro Finance company, was given licence to float a full fledged Commercial Bank. Mr. Chahandra Sekhar Ghosh, the founder of Bandhan, has created for himself a big name in the new age Retail Banking history.

This is the story of how gradually a host of banks made their foray into Retail Banking world to service the bottom most earning group in the pyramid of the population and how to a huge population of about 30 Crores the banking facilities was opened. As these Small Finance Banks got access to public deposits lowering their cost of fund and reducing dependability on investors, we find a little concern. While these banks are no threat to establish PSU and Private sector banks, there is a strong competition among these ten banks to enter the Liability market whether in urban or rural areas. This competition and desperation to capture the market often forces certain banks to hike up their deposit rates to allure customers. This becomes unhealthy and is a serious concern for those banks who are in this game .

Let us peep into the BPL households to gather an idea about the life style of the people in that segment. During my two years of association I had an opportunity to get in touch with those people in the so called Urban Poor community. MFIs extends group loans mainly to the women since there is an observation that ladies are far more sincere than male members as far as repayment is concerned.

The following two stories may throw some light on the life style of the MFI target segment :

When I had joined one of the leading MFIs in Kolkata, I noticed that death rate of the women borrowers was abnormally high. Initially I had a doubt that most of these were fraud cases to avoid loan repayment or to extract money from Insurance companies. In big branches of banks the incidents of death is may be 7 to 9 in a year whereas, I found that this figure was as high as 10 to 25 in a year in a branch. I was curious and ordered a probe. What came out is a crude reality in the BPL community. I found all the death cases were genuine and the reasons are painful like (a) Mal nutrition (b) Incurable diseases, (c) Lack of peace in the family where the women who work hard to maintain their families are regularly beaten by drunkard husbands e.t.c.

As MFIs give business loans to women in group of 5 to 9, there is a group leader in every group and in her house weekly / fortnightly meetings are held. *I, as part of my job, visited few such households where people live in one room. The kitchen is accommodated in that 10/12 Ft room. A small space is allotted for the gods and goddesses. There is no cupboard also to keep the clothes. These are kept generally in iron trunks which are placed under the cot. Sometimes few valuable sarees which are worn in special occasions, are hung from a string tied from one wall to the other. The borrowing members assemble in that room and sit on the floor and discuss their problems with the MFI representatives who collect instalments and give receipts.*

This is the world of the lowest line of social pyramid. With the formation of ten Small Finance Banks it is expected that the country will go ahead with their mission for Financial Inclusion and the regulatory control will help this huge population in accessing banking facilities not only in obtaining financial assistance at reasonable cost but also to safe keep their hard earned money with their bankers.

HUMAN
RESOURCE
And
RETAIL BANK

WHO ARE THE ARCHITECTS OF BUSINESS?

Before taking our readers for a walk through the orchard of Human Resource in Retail Banking world, here are few lines dedicated to the People – who are the architect of business.

"Though your balance sheet is a model of what balance sheets should be;
Typed and ruled with great precision in a type that all can see;
Though the grouping of the assets is commendable and clear;
And the details which are given more than usually appear;
Though investments have been valued at the scale price of the day;
And the auditor's certificate shows everything O.K.;
One asset is omitted, and it's worth I want to know;
The asset is the Value of the men, who run the show."

In fact the key note of this part of the book, I feel, is those above lines.

The competition in the financial sectors is gradually increasing with the increase in the economy of the third world countries. This has given rise to the demand of the talent pool in order to be at par with the demand of productivity and business growth which contributes to the bottom lines. The significance of Human Resource has gradually gone to its peak since it is one of the essential factors behind the image and the affluence of an organisation.

Retail Banking is a vast field involving at least 700 Mio of banking population in India. Its wings, its multi front activities, its technology and missions are altogether different from other industries or other verticals in the banking system. It needs and necessarily involves people in large scale. Looks rather simple, Human Resource management is of a complex nature. Success of Retail Bank majorly depends on how Human Resource is skilfully handled in the organization. Like its customers, the big group of human resource is also driven by human psychology which is to be taken into account all through the process of HR management.

If we take up a sample size of 200 employees from different banks across all levels, we will be acquainted with the huge diversity in this world of population with diverse mindset, skills, education. They join this industry afresh or as a lateral entrant. It is also interesting to observe how, with time, various changes are wrought in them driven mostly by psychology.

It is a complex planet and for Retail Bank to grow, human resource needs to be adroitly handled with care, sympathy and empathy.

Let us look at the areas where Human Resource is involved in running Retail Bank vertical:

- ✓ Talent and Talent Management
- ✓ Talent acquisition / Retention / Attrition
- ✓ Performance management
- ✓ Reward and Recognition
- ✓ Learning and Development
- ✓ Employee Satisfaction

TALENT and TALENT MANAGEMENT

Talent management is increasingly seen as a critical success factor as organisations strive to meet their customers' needs innovatively, efficiently and effectively. However, careful consideration must be given to the development and implementation of talent management for it to be successful.

What is Talent?

Definition of talent can vary across organisations, for example:

- A transnational organisation may define talent as the top-performing 1% of executives.
- Another organisation could define talent as the top 10% of high-performers, whatever their role or level.
- Yet another may have a 'mix', defining talent not only as executives with potential for board-level appointments, but also high-potential individuals who are identified as the leaders of tomorrow.
- Some may be taking an end-to-end view of newly appointed graduates to top leadership.
- Finally, some might take the view that every employee should be included in talent management activities.

Talent Acquisition

At this point where it is immensely important for an organisation to recruit the right people for the right profile, poaching is also becoming a usual practice. With a number of booming financial industries, be it Insurance, Retail Banks or Micro Finance sectors, the talent economy is left with numerous options to choose from (Ford et. al, 2010).

Modern Retail Banks induct such talent from various sources:

1. From Management institutions through campus interviews.
2. From other banks and organizations as mid-careers.

Fresh management students are recruited, trained, placed on the job and pushed through career path over a period of time. These groups enter the Retail banks with energy, vigour and aspirations.

The second group of people enter or switch over to banks with their age old experience and skills in various verticals. They generally fill in vacancies in middle or top management and contribute to the growth of their organization. Now both the groups are driven by two different mindsets.

Many fresh talents who get recruited in the banks with a high ambition to climb the ladder often get impatient and within a short period start exploring opportunities outside. This was faced by Standard Chartered in mid 90s when a flock of young MBAs and CAs joined the bank with high energies and initiatives. Within a couple of years many of them lost their interest and tried to switch over to other banks. At one point, the bank decided not only to depend on IIM graduates. Their focus shifted to creating a mix with people from Tier II institutes since it was observed that officers from the Tier II Management centres tend to stick longer and give their best.

As regards recruitment of mid-careers, people in the age group of 32 to 40 tend to settle down with their bags of experiences. However, in Retail Bank scenario, they create a demand in the market over a period of time and instead of actively job hunting they are open to responding to calls from competitor banks.

For new generation banks there is a different and interesting story. As soon as banks like HDFC, UTI, ICICI had launched their platforms on the soil, they also rushed to an acquisition spree and started recruiting across levels. With the fast organic expansion employees in this green field were getting elevations at an unusual speed. As regards HDFC Bank, the Personnel committee used to meet every quarter to discuss performance and elevations. There were employees who had enjoyed two to three elevations in a year. But a time passed this initial speed of recruitment and elevation became slow to slower mainly because of ground level employees growing in experience and more mid careers joining. We found numerous in-flows from foreign banks this time for higher positions and also to avoid stagnation in their existing banks. This led to impatience, if not frustration, among those people who were enjoying quick elevations over two / three years.

This change generated a reaction among the banks. We found the following movement:

- ➢ Juniors turned skilled through experience and training. They found demand for themselves and started testing their market.
- ➢ Competitor banks started recruiting trained young blood with experience.
- ➢ As a reaction, the loser bank went ahead to snatch resources from competition and thus Poaching started which became a cyclic order.
- ➢ In the upper ranks too we found the same picture of poaching and switching over loyalty.
- ➢ One new phenomenon was surfaced and this is called **"Herd Mentality"**. Seasoned employee with leadership quality and renowned in the circuit is recruited by a bank from the competition and the same person joins the new organization along with skilled team. Surprisingly, this is encouraged by his new employer. The small team then combines with the new group in the new platform. It's like a flock of sheep following a sheep from one pasture to a newer one. While we understand that the leader has high credibility and capability, sometimes things may go wrong perchance something goes wrong with the leader.
- ➢ Again, it is observed poaching has its own set of cons as well. Ultimately the banks suffer in the cyclic order of poaching and filling in vacancies. They recruit people, train them, nurture in the organization and one day a competitor bank lifts them up with higher pay package. To bridge the gaps the loser bank goes to the market and recruits with higher pay from some other bank and their costs shoots up. When an employee changes his/her

organization, the switch involves usually with a pay hike of 25 to 30% if not more and often with a grade jump. Again the bank recruiting the same person takes a load on cost of Human Resource. Thus, through this game of poaching and recruiting, banks shoulder additional cost as their investments in Learning and Development goes to toss. The employees, on the other hand, benefit themselves with pay hikes and grade jump.

➤ But within a couple of years there was a reverse scenario. People who joined the new generation banks and were enjoying elevations and financial benefits in quick succession, soon found stagnation in career progression. After an unpremeditated speed in career, they found themselves in a "No Vacancy" position.

Employee Turnover

Employee turnover, in this context, refers to the percentage or number of worker who quit an organization and consequently replaced with new ones (Mathis & Jackson, 2012). A high staff turnover is said to have a significant effect on the bottom line of organizations of all sizes. Since satisfied employees usually don't give up on their jobs, high staff turnover is often indicative of an organizational problem.

Types of employee turnover

In a number of instances, employee turnover has received a negative connotation; a sigma attributed to an employer's responsibility to minimize staff turnover at all costs. However, literature confirms the existence of distinct types of staff turnover, some of which are not negative. Mathis & Jackson (2012) identifies three different categories that employee turnover can take, with each category having two non-mutually exclusive types of turnover.

- ## Voluntary verses Involuntary Turnover

Voluntary turnover arises when employees quit an organization voluntarily (by choice). According to Mathis & Jackson (2012) voluntary employee turnover often results from factors like job dissatisfaction, change of residency, seeking career opportunities in other firms, family reasons, pay and beneficial reasons, and other factors. Research reveals that there is a positive correlation between voluntary employee turnover and the size of an organization, with large firms being less effectual in preventing employee turnover (Mathis & Jackson, 2012). Involuntary turnover occurs when employees at all levels of an organization are terminated by employers for a number of issues (mostly functional) such as changes in organizational policies, excessive absenteeism, failure to meet performance standards and code of ethics, and violations of work rules.

- ## Functional verses Dysfunctional Turnover

Not all employee turnovers are negative to an organization. Some workforce losses may be considered as being desirable, especially when nonperforming, disruptive, and /or less reliable workers quit an organization. This type of employee turnover is functional turnover which represents an affirmative change (Mathis & Jackson, 2012). However, if high performers and key individuals leave the organization at critical times, operational stagnation may arise abruptly. This type of turnover is therefore regarded as dysfunctional turnover.

- ## Controllable verses uncontrollable turnover

Studies reveal that workers leave organizations for multiple reasons: some controllable while others may be outside the scope of an organization control. Uncontrollable employee turnover may occur from factors such as change of employee's geographical area, family issues, among others (Mathis & Jackson, 2012).

Causes of Employee Turnover

While discussing the attrition part of the employees, it may be pertinent to run through a very important question - Why people leave organizations? For any Retail Bank where turnover is very high, it is pertinent for the management to know the reasons for which their employees quit. When good employees leave, productivity sinks, morale suffers and colleagues struggle with increased workload. Add in recruitment and training costs, and on boarding new hires can make for a difficult and expensive transition.

The best solution is to keep the workers happy so they don't leave. But before the organization implements a plan to increase employee retention, they need to determine why valuable employees are leaving.

Several reasons have been identified as being central in facilitating high employee turnover in organizations. First, it is clear that a mismatch between the job and the employee's skills can trigger employee turnover. This scenario can be traced to employees who are assigned tasks that are too complex for their skills. Moreover, if the skills of employees are underutilized in the job, they may be discouraged and quit the organization. Another possible cause of employee turnover is unfavourable working conditions (Armstrong, 2010). For instance, if employees' working conditions lack standard or important facilities such as restrooms, furniture, proper lighting, health and safety provisions, most of them may not be willing to stay long.

Below is a list of most common reasons employees jump ship to new employers:

1. Superior-Subordinate Relationship

Superiors are inseparable part for employees in their professional lives. Superiors provide direction and advices on one to one basis. They provide feedback on performance from time to time and act as a bridge to the senior management. They are the major reasons to why an employee severe relationship with the organization. It is rightly said that employees do not leave organizations, they leave their Bosses.

At the same time, a Boss may be good and efficient in his own place but the subordinate may not be able to live up to the expectation of his Boss. In such case neither the Superior is satisfied with the performance of the subordinate, nor is the subordinate able to understand his shortcomings. Where can this lead to?

Here is an example - *This happened when my boss was reporting to our Managing Director who, over a period of time was disillusioned with my boss. This was evident in his gestures and behaviour towards my boss. My superior was inducted from a NBFC climate and could not connect with banking culture and expectations. One day during lunch at a nearby restaurant he had expressed to me, "I am not comfortable. Not able to face my boss. Generally, in the morning everyone opens the mails of bosses, but I panic at the first sight of his name in my inbox. I don't feel like going to office in the morning and sometimes shiver as I wake up".* This is a sad situation and often affects an employee with no big fault of his boss.

2. No Excitement in Work creates Boredom

Work place is more than half of our world. It needs to be exciting else monotony captures the individual since an employee is a human being and not a robotic element. As none likes an unchallenged life, a bored employee starts looking for greener pastures in quest of light and air. Work for any employee is a passion and if the passion for performance is absent, loyalty gets switched to competition.

Hence it is important to ensure that each employee is engaged with passion and excitement. Working closely with them is a solution to identify the issue and resolve it.

3. Colleagues and Relationship

At the time of bidding good bye to the organization, people write farewell letters placing the good time on record and the kind treatment they have received from colleagues. Often these notes are superficial and tears and agonies are hidden behind. Sometimes employees leave due to conflicts in the work place and when it is unmanageable for them. Silently they quit without blaming anybody. This is dangerous for the organization since due to lack of vigilance a good hand may be lost to competition. A good atmosphere in the organization and support from the co-workers often make an employee reverse the decision of leaving the company. End of it every employee should feel his organization "A best place to work".

4. Application of Skills and Abilities

Employees always look for opportunities to apply their acquired, knowledge, skills and abilities. Once they get this opportunity, a sense of pride and satisfaction is generated. This motivates them to perform higher resulting in contribution to the organization. Ultimately their skills and knowledge are expanded leading to a greater boost to their self confidence to the tangible benefits of the organization.

If the reverse happens where an employee's skills are redundant, dissatisfaction grows shrinking the opportunity that he/she looks for. If this state of affair continues and management is reluctant to identify the gap to resolve, the individual is engulfed with frustration and ultimately looks for a change. In this process, the company is at a loss. A timely remedy can avoid such exit and a clearly defined career path for the individual can retain the skill within the organization.

5. Contribution to Overall Mission of the Organization

Every employee should be made crystal clear about his/ her roles and responsibilities and his/her contribution to the Financial and non-financial goals of his organization. This brings a strong sense of belongingness and enhances the sense of ownership. This pushes the performance of the employee affecting the growth of the company positively. If this does not happen, employees feel detached with the mainstream of the organization and lose interest in their work place. If they feel that they are not part of the larger picture of the organization the oneness with their company is defeated and a good team work cannot be built.

6. Empowerment in Work Place

Empowerment has been found to be an essential part of employee satisfaction and a chained employee will not like to work as a puppet in his/her own place. This is one of the many reasons for which exits happen.

7. Weak Health of Organization

Financial instability in any organization gives birth to layoffs, freezing of pay hike, hiring. Bad media publicities, higher attrition of colleagues, uncertainty due to merger and acquisition all together throw an employee to a sense of insecurity resulting in stress. A worried employee, a stressed staff will never like to stick to his/her organization and will switch over to other boat at the earliest opportunity.

In such condition any organization may face exit in a mass thus leading to a major crises. To avoid such a situation, higher transparency is required which should bring all individuals into confidence through clear communication of the true status of the company. This creates trust among the employees in their management team and majority of them end up lending hands to their company to surmount crises.

8. Recognition of Job Performance

As is human nature, every individual likes to be recognized and rewarded for their contribution to the organization. Management's endeavour is to give credit where it's due thus retaining good hands. In every organization we come across instances of people being disgruntled over the assessment of their performance. Such employees look out as soon as they find opportunities.

Hence, to retain performing employees, management needs to focus on their reward and recognition program which must run religiously without bias.

As regards leaving existing organization, another tendency is often observed. This comes out of continuous dissatisfaction over present state in the organization whether position or package or rewards. In many cases we witness employees testing their marketability by appearing for interview in other banks. When they receive a good offer, they approach their present employers and inform them of the new offer directly or indirectly pressurizing for pay hike or promotion. This is opportunism for sure but given the job market scenario employers, one cannot call this action 'unjustified' as well.

It is thus important to stay in constant touch with individual employees and fathom their mind. The bank needs to know whether their employees are happy, do they find delight in their job and their responsibilities meaningful? To retain good employees, this is of paramount importance. More the bank keeps in touch with their employees, more is the opportunity to ease out retention issues.

Retention

This situation led the banks to adopt two pronged strategy. Primarily, they felt it necessary to retain the existing talents. As per plan the following actions were found:

The new generation banks started introducing Employees' Stock Option Plan (ESOP) for officers in higher ranks where the beneficiaries would have to serve the bank at least for 3 years. This provision was given to people who were identified as High Potential individuals. In some banks employees in lower ranks were also given such options very selectively. In this Wealth Creation scheme high performing staff stopped thinking of "Sun Shine outside".

In some banks the management floated "Retention Bonus" thus allotting hefty amount of standalone and onetime bonus with a 3 year retention clause.

Thus when banks found it difficult to offer promotional avenues due to traffic jam, they wanted to hold back their precious employees with financial allurement. It worked.

Gone are the days when employees used to stick to one organisation for a lifetime. Now we often find employees switching loyalty, changing jobs according to their preferences adding status and financial values to their lives. As discussed above, these reasons range from better pay package, career development and promotion options, scope of training and development, psychological rewards to name a few. Needless to say, investing huge time and effort in designing a retention strategy, too has become a top priority for a human resource professional. This is because recruiting new staff involves sizeable amount of expense than retaining them. The investments go in induction, training and nurturing them through a substantial period of time. The pay package itself costs at least 20-30% more than the package benefitted by the exiting employee. Thus, in order to avoid this, organisations should have effective retention strategy.

Inability on the organization's part to retain employees indicates poor management and a lack of good planning (Ramlall, 2004). This can be done by ensuring optimum job satisfaction for the employees without compromising on the business. Hence job satisfaction becomes a key factor which goes hand in hand with retention. A higher satisfaction of employees with their jobs and the organisation they work for will lead them to hold on to the organization since the choices will be very less (Hausknecht et. Al, 2008).

The increased number of acquisitions and merging among organizations in various industries has left workers haunted with the fear of losing their jobs. Employees thus have come up with career move strategies to ensure that their job security is intact. On the other hand, employers have come up with the platform of ensuring that their current workers are discouraged from moving to other organizations. One of the key factors that facilitate employee retention is Employee Development Programs. Logan (2000) argues that through offering this program, organizations are in a position of boycotting hiring and retraining expenses of new employees. The axiom "good help is hard to find" has been tested to be true because of the increased tightness of the job market (Eskildesen and Nussler, 2000).

According to Davidow and Uttal (1989), effective retention ensures that offering employee development programs costs less as compared to hiring new talents. This is because the management is already aware of the wants and desires of the existing employees as the cost of attracting new workers keeps on rising.

Who is responsible for retention?

Following the studies given above, leaders and managers should be given first hand responsibility in killing unwanted attrition in organizations. Now the question is how does this relate to many leaders or managers' belief systems?

Many managers believe that the loss of talented employees is because of external factors. These external factors include non-competitive benefits and compensation, acquisitions or merger, lack of instigating corporate leadership, and economic related realties. Other top management parties believe that the key reason for low rates of retention resides behind the bars of Human Reason departments (Coetzee, 2007).

Managers assume that their responsibilities include their own job roles, attending meetings, and projects to complete. They forget the two key factors which have the most impact on retention. These include employee development schemes and career coaching as well as keeping strong relationship and loyalty, which makes employee feel motivated and enthusiastic to live and grow with the company (Batten, 1991).

Effective employee retention strategy criteria

As revealed by various literatures, it is clear that employees are the most valuable assets of an organization, since they contribute significantly to effective running of the day-to-day operations of a business (Marquis & Huston, 2009). Despite of its many benefits, selecting an inappropriate retention strategy may not yield expected results. In determining an effective retention strategy, HR managers need to consider some set criteria.

- **Degree of cost reduction**

  An effective employee retention strategy must be capable of significantly reducing organization costs associated with talent acquisition and hiring, and employee training and development. The lesser these costs are, the more effective the retention strategy. The hiring costs of new employees include interview costs, the costs of posting jobs on media, and even the opportunity costs time wasted in hiring new employees (Stratton, 2011). Even for those firms that use agents to hire new staff, agency fees often form part of their annual employee wages. Interviewing costs arise owing to the fact that in large companies, there are some departments whose primary responsibility is to screen and interview new talents. In some cases, employees from other departments may be assigned extra responsibility to participate in the hiring process. The time those individual consume in screening, reviewing and scrutinizing resumes draws them away from their key job responsibility, resulting to low job productivity and potential opportunity costs (Mathis & Jackson, 2012).

In most organizations, new staff members often undergo a comprehensive training programme on organizational culture, ethics, values, office practices, and on specific job skills (Regis, 2009). Just like hiring, the training process of new employees requires the participation of current employees in educating the new staff on the way a business carries out its business. This also takes the current employees away from their job responsibilities. Kaila (2005) asserts an effective employee retention strategy should not only reduce an organization's training costs but should also improve the returns on investment that an organization made in their training.

- **Degree with which the strategy reduces employee turnover**

One of the key goals of staff retention strategies is to minimize staff turnover. Thus, an effective employee retention strategy should be capable of making considerable reductions to an organization's staff turnover rates. Literature postulates that an effective staff retention strategy should aid an organization in developing a pool of high skilled workforce (Fenny, 2008). By working in teams or individually for a long period, employees have been found to share expertise and knowledge regarding their job responsibilities, which in turn improves their aggregate efficiency in the work environment. In addition, it is argued that an affective retention strategy should be capable of increasing the existing employees' commitment to continued expansion of originality, creating and quality in the workplace (Stahl & Morris, 2012).

- **Degree with which the strategy elevates the level of customer satisfaction**

  Customers are one of the key stakeholders of any business enterprise. In this regard, with the current increasing competition in the global business environment, organizations have found it beneficial to provide high quality customer service in order to increase customer loyalty. Researchers have identified a positive correlation between staff retention and organization's level of customer satisfaction fuelled by service quality and employee relationship with customers. Wulf et al (1997) confirms that an effective employee staff retention strategy must be capable of improving the quality of customer services in an organization. In his book "Customer Service Action Plan Instructor Guide", he states that a better customer service can solely be offered by competent and qualified staff. For a firm to consistently provide exceptional customer service, retention strategies are crucial: it must hire, frequently train, and regularly reward customer-oriented staff.

Attrition

At the end, as a natural process, every organization finds the accumulation of under or non-performing employees over a period of time. This increases cost and hence as part of process a bank needs to periodically eliminate such employees from the system. Gone are those days when Voluntary Retirement Schemes were floated with approval of Government of India and people were to be convinced to leave.

Now that most of these new generation banks don't suffer from the intervention of trade union bodies, they have the free hand to ask the unwanted employees to leave with a notice period. A German bank, in my knowledge, asks such employees to leave the premises within few hours lock, stock and barrel. 'Hire and Fire' has thus become part and parcel of organizations.

In a high demanding environment in Retail Banks often people find it difficult to satisfy the management with desired output in business. This is seen especially in the cases of Branch Heads and Relationship Managers. Often for reasons beyond their control these people are marked non-performers. However, the HR pie is the costliest expense areas for any bank and jointly the business segment and HR vertical ensure that Attrition happens in a smooth way so that Human Resource cost of the vertical is justified.

Work-Life Balance:

Baltes (1999) suggests that job sharing, flexible timings, shorter work weeks and telecommuting are some of the elements affecting job satisfaction. Work-life balance policies helps the employees to get the stress off them since it eases family demands and helps them to balance both professional and personal life easily. This reduces absenteeism and turnover and boosts retention since the employees feel the organization values their wishes to pursue their own interests too turnover (Landauer, 1997).

Redundancy

During the 90s when Retail Banking started in India, there was high demand of talent –both fresher and experienced. But over a period of time, say two decades, the scenario changed slowly. The question of cost came to the forefront, accountabilities were questioned, skill sets came under scanner and the need for attrition was felt. In this process, it became a regular affair when people were being asked to find other avenues. This gave rise to insecurity and on the other hand also opened up opportunities. Redundancy, followed by attrition, brings balance in work force enhancing the overall quality of the team while competition starts hiring trained people to cover their gaps. Even if one person is found redundant in one bank, the same may be found fit in another.

LEARNING AND DEVELOPMENT

Training is among the key factors used for employee retention. According to United States Department of Labour (2009), job training enables employees' personal behaviour and professional development. Access of an employee to training and development programs enables the organization in facilitating organizational growth in terms of technology and performance improvements (Boomer Authority, 2009). According to Prenda and Stahl (2001), cost saving programs and organizational benefits associated with training programs outweigh expenses incurred.

With the fast expansion in the galaxy of Retail Banking the need for Learning and Development (L&D) is being felt very seriously. Sincerity is THE NEED, but is not all. Industrious habit is essential but is not all. What is important is to build a strong and skilled team with adequate knowledge and experience to cope up with the accelerated growth of a technology driven business vertical. And, for that any Retail Bank should be on their toes to create an efficient L&D team who will drive the mission with success. What are the steps?

> ➢ To scan the existing skill, knowledge and motivation level of the individuals and also of the team.
> ➢ To identify the gaps between existing and required skills, knowledge and motivation.
> ➢ To determine the Training and Learning need for each and every individual staff.
> ➢ To draw career graph and progression for each one of them.
> ➢ To arrange for adequate Training facilities with skilled trainers, in-house or out sourced.

➤ To methodically follow the Developments and take corrective measures.

➤ To identify those employees who cannot keep pace with others and are the back benchers.

The above activities of L&D team will support the HR teams in their Retention and Attrition exercise. It will help them to tag individual employees in any of the following categories :

- Hi-potential
- Potential
- Low potential
- Keeping afloat
- Needs removal

Einsen (2005) argues that organizations with training programs experiences 70% increase in employee retention. He further argues that organizations that includes advancement opportunities, career challenges, competitive employee benefits, work incentives, and supportive working climate in their training programs experience effective retention strategies regardless of their (employees) age. Studies support that effective training programs enhances prosperity, growth, and retention for both the employees and employers (Amble, 2006). According to McIntosh (2001) and Berryman & Vaughan (1989), there is a positive relationship between enhanced training basements like efficiencies, competencies, and intelligence, and highly developed practices, mentoring, cross training, technology and mentoring chances for every employee. Both tangible and intangible training benefits draw a parallel connection with high levels of competency, consistency, adaptability, productivity, loyalty, and independency in worker at any given age (Yazinski, 2009; Boomer Authority, 2009; Agrela, 2008).

Accordingly the HR vertical, as a support service team will give feedback to business segment for further course of action. This process is of paramount importance to build and maintain a balanced team for Retail Bank to prosper with health.

PERFORMANCE MANAGEMENT

Definition of Performance Management

- Getting better results from the organization, teams and individuals by understanding and managing performance within an agreed framework of planned goals, standards and attribute/competence requirements (Armstrong 1994).
- A systematic approach to improving individual and team performance in order to achieve organizational goals... the approach you take should depend on your organization: its culture, its relationship with employees and the types of jobs they do (Hendry et al 1997).

Before going deep into this chapter, we may look at what, according to many, is meant by performance:

Quite a vague concept and people often leave the field half way before they can clarify it. However, we often hear people say that <u>Individual Performance</u> can be interpreted as expressing the relationship between a person's capabilities, i.e. what someone is capable of doing, and what the person actually achieves.

Again, Productivity is a concept that links the inputs to a production process to outputs, expressed in quantitative or financial terms. Applied to the individual, it is very close to performance. Let us be acquainted with certain terms used in measuring performance.

- <u>Efficiency</u> is a term that is used to explain how well resources/people are used. It is often associated with "Doing things right".
- <u>Effectiveness</u> describes the relationship between targets/ objectives set, the behaviour we engage in to meet these targets and what is actually achieved. "Doing the right thing".
- <u>Effort</u> – a difficult concept but often linked to the intensity of work; how hard you work, but not necessarily linked to outcomes.
- <u>Effort Bargain</u> is a concept that links performance to reward.

The purpose of **employee focus performance** is to integrate and link together individual goals, departmental purposes and organizational objectives. The aim is to share understanding about what is to be achieved and also to provide the support and guidance to teams and individuals towards continuous improvement of business processes. **What are, then, the intended outcomes of Performance Management?**

- Control
- Reward
- Motivation
- Development or Assessment

The next question that comes is what Performance Management can control? It enables a Retail Bank to monitor the 'effort' that an employee makes to earn their reward and also to assess contribution to outputs – financial, sales, improved customer relationships, speed etc. Performance Management measures effective behaviours – achievement of service standards, completion of activities, supporting values, innovation, etc. It does also re-enforce corporate values.

Unless a Retail Bank management accurately manages the performance of the vertical, all efforts become fruitless. As the financial year moves, the Retail Bank core team must evaluate the performance periodically and assess the progress and health. However, it goes without saying that performance of the Retail Bank is directly linked with the performance of its employees whether in group or at individual level. Hence, both business and HR verticals need to ensure that performance of a team or an individual staff is measured and tracked. It is said that what cannot be measured, cannot be assessed. Hence to measure the performance of an employee a yard stick or method is necessary. The latest method used is called **Balanced Score Card**. Let us see how it works.

What is Balanced Score Card ?

The balanced scorecard (BSC) is a strategic planning and management system that organizations use to:

- Communicate what they are trying to accomplish
- Align the day-to-day work that everyone is doing with strategy
- Prioritize projects, products, and services
- Measure and monitor progress towards strategic targets

The Balanced Scorecard Links Performance Measures

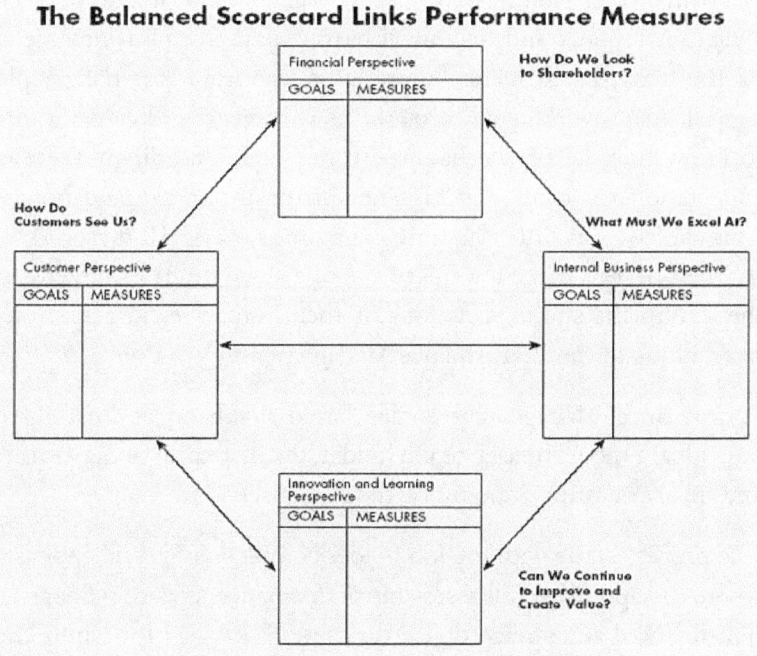

While the organization, as a whole, or the Retail Bank as a vertical needs to measure their performance on various fronts, one of the key parts is measuring the performance of its Human Resource. Key Result Areas (KRA) are thus designed for each position in the vertical. KRA includes both financial and non-financial objectives that an employee needs to achieve.

KRA also indicates the percentage of weightage against each area of responsibilities that the concerned member is to follow throughout the year with performance. Thus individual performance leads to group performance which ends with the overall performance of the organization or the vertical. Thus as Business moves, the Human Resource structure should go through Performance exercise for their resources to determine and record how the team is faring both at individual and collective levels. For any Retail Bank who handles a very sizeable number of people at various levels and on multiple business fronts, it is a big task where Performance appraisals of every individual are ideally done twice a year, half yearly and on annual basis. Apart from business need of the bank, Performance appraisal is important for the people as well. After working all through the year, every individual wants to know how he or she has performed and accordingly there is expectation for change in his /her financial package and bonus. This exercise, is a little elaborate in nature as every HR division will try their best to make it a full proof one since it relates directly to the sentiments and expectations of their human resources. Let us have a look at the Performance Management:

Performance Management is tier based involving at least three individuals, the Appraisee or job holder, the Appraiser or Supervisor and third one is the Superior of the Appraiser.

The process starts with the Job holder completing his self appraisal where the appraisee will assess his performance, covering financial, non-financial and stretch objectives as per KRAs set for him in the beginning of the year. The job holder will not only post self ratings in different areas of responsibility, he will have to justify each of his rating.

In the next phase the appraisal form goes to the supervisor who is expected to examine the self appraisal of his reportee and assess the veracity as wee as justification given there in. The appraiser will rate in each section and will find out a suitable time to sit with the job holder for a discussion. Ideally this process should allow enough time and opportunity to the job holder to defend his case. Once the appraiser explains to the appraise his own opinion about the self appraisal and also explains where all the job holder excels and where are the short coming, he/she will give the Overall Rating which is generally best of 4. The qualitative descriptions are Excellent, Very Good, Fair and Below the Standard. The meeting should end with the satisfaction of the job holder over the assessment.

Appraisal exercise does not end here and the form goes to the next higher level, generally one up where the senior person will have a look at the appraisal and, if necessary, will discuss the ratings with the appraiser. The form moves to Human Resource vertical from the business division.

THE TOUGH PHASE

The HR division gets appraisal forms from all the sections of Retail Bank and sort those out according to the Ratings. Generally the departmental heads or the appraisers are advised to take care of the Ratings. They are in following distribution pattern :

Excellent	- 10%
Very Good	- 20%
Fair	- 60%
Below Standard	- 10%

Very often the appraisers cannot maintain the percentage in the top two categories where the Reward factor comes. It is a common problem that is faced by a number of appraisers who need to run his platform with this performing team in the following financial year and since he is the leader. But when it comes to the organization as a whole, there is a different problem in the Rating exercise. The name of the problem is **Bell Curve.** Let us peep into this window to understand this unique problem:

Bell Curve

While managing finance of the total bank, the CFO and other business heads need to determine the amount that the bank is willing to spend for Increment and Bonus for the year. There is an inner and an outer limit in this budget. The range of percentage of increment to various Rate holders is also looked at. Accordingly instructions are sent to all the regions, branches and department to adhere to the percentage in Ratings. And the Appraisers fail to comply with this due to various reasons like (1) Personal relations with certain good employees (2) Too many good staff in the team and very difficult to make few of them unhappy (3) Skill and efficiency difference between two are very narrow etc. These are on humanitarian ground which cannot be evaded so easily. But, end of it, the organization has a total purse and they cannot over spend. Here comes the term Bell Curve which connotes "Forced Rating". When the HR vertical reports that the percentage has jumped over the determined number in top two slots, bank goes back to the departments asking the supervisors to down grade some staff to arrive at the stipulated number when a unique problem appears. After the first round of appraisal exercise between the job holder and the appraiser, the job holder leaves with a certain impression that he has been rated, say, 1. But when Bell Curve is applied, it is not done in his presence. At best his supervisor is consulted and finally informed of the down rating. This is eventually passed on to the job holder with an excuse that he was given 1 as per appraisal but it was found that he ranks at the lower level when compared with other 1 rated colleagues of him. This definitely upsets those victims of Bell Curving but that is the story.

Reward and Recognition

Higher recognition for achievement and a good reward programme increases employee satisfaction since they feel valued and appreciated. This makes them more dedicated and loyal to the organization and the job role. Appreciation by colleagues and supervisor too contributes to job satisfaction and employee retention (Mohrman et al., 1996; Cunningham et al., 1996; Bushe et al., 1996).

After the successful completion of Bell Curving, the bank is ready to fix increments for the people. Generally increments are given in the following manner and ranges :

Excellent	- 13 to 14%
Very Good	- 10 to 12 %
Fair	- 7 to 9 %
Below Standard	- No increment

Once the employees come to know what Rating they have been given, the part related to rate of increment is not so problematic. People are mentally prepared with calculations. In the next phase the question of Bonus comes and as per practice, there is no question of giving bonus to the employees in the last two categories. Here the Retail Bank management needs to decide who all are the "Must Retain" staff members and who are the high performing members that can be let go if situation occurs. Accordingly, the kitty allotted to the segment is distributed among people carrying 1 and 2 ratings. Usually it is seen that people in the T-1 category get the bigger portions of the cakes and more so, staff in the Business front. A trend is also seen that employees in the back office or support services are not often highly favoured in case of bonus allocation. Banks are found to be more kind towards people who are directly connected to business and generate the same. However, in the total process of Performance Management one section of employees are seen happy, another group are also "not unhappy" and get ready to fight out in the next round. People in the third group who are left to "Keep Afloat", are confused about what to do and how to improve and the last section marked as "Below Standard" start suffering from insecurity in the work place and find out job to save themselves.

There are two other parts in the Reward and Recognition area. The first is "Golden Handcuff" which is meant for those high performing employees whom the bank wants to retain at least for three years. These performing employees are allotted ESOPs with a minimum retention clause of three years. This ensures Talent retention and what is left is Elevation.

Whether for expansion of business or vacancies arising out of attrition, the bank needs to elevate people from various ranks and position them in those places. Here, again the question of choice comes and obviously the best fitted candidates are chosen for the best interest of business. This is another way that an efficient employee gets recognized and rewarded in terms of promotion.

In spite of the Reward and Recognition programs banks find attrition in two ways :

a) Almost immediately after the increment is declared and bonus is disbursed, a set of performing employees leave the organization using the increment letters and using the shift for a grade or positional elevation.

b) The second set of staff who are unhappy with the financial changes will look for greener pastures and find a new boat to start new innings.

c) The Non-performers, on the other hand, become desperate to find shelter sensing that any day the organization may issue marching order.

The life comes back to normal and the organization needs to get set for another yearly journey. But at this juncture, what is required is to run the team injecting motivation into them and with skills redefined for the new mission and vision. Here comes the L&D team with new plans and calendar to conduct year long activities. To cope up with the market development, innovation of new product, new sales strategies to tackle competition the bank must upgrade skills of employees in an ongoing basis. L&D ensures involving both in house and outsourced trainers for this purpose. While the line managers are best choice for training in operations, products e.t.c, the outsourced faculties handle the soft skills like sales, customer care e.t.c.

LEADERSHIP

According to Ismail et al. (2010), the two most important leadership styles are participative and consultative which helps indirectly in organizational commitment and positively correlated to job satisfaction. Hence, to address the saying "people leave managers and not companies", organizations should encourage a transparent leadership approach.

In any retail bank where involvement of human resource is on a larger scale and where the total resource are split into a number of sub-sections yet they need to work together, Leadership is most vital. Every individual, driving a team – small or big, must be a leader in his own place and it should be his effort to graduate himself from a Manager to a Leader. Let us see what the world think about Leadership. In one sentence Leadership is Leading people, Influencing people, Commanding people and Guiding people.

"Management is about arranging & telling. Leadership is about nurturing & enhancing."

(Thomas J. Peters)

This is the glimpse of the difference that we get from Thomas J. Peters. It states clear that there is a marked difference between a Manager and a Leader. And Keith Davis goes a step ahead to say, Leadership is "The ability to persuade others to seek defined objectives". It is easily understandable that unless a Manager prepares himself as a leader, the desired goal of nurturing and building a team towards achievement of goals is not possible. To look at this more clearly, Leadership is to influence a group to achieve the goal whereas Management is use of inherent authority in designated formal rank to obtain compliance from people down the line. To be more clear about the difference between the two roles let us look below:

A Manager

- Appointed
- Wields Authority
- Administer
- Maintain
- Control
- Short-term view
- Ask how and when
- Initiate
- Accept the status quo
- Do things right

A True Leader

- Emerges
- Wields Power
- Innovate
- Develop
- Inspire
- Long-term view
- Ask what and why
- Originate
- Challenge the status quo
- Do the right thing

Since being a Leader is important for any Manager to successfully drive his team to desired destination and for any Retail Bank building leaders in the team only enrich the team. Since in Retail Banks Leaders are there at various levels, the following diagram may throw light on the skills that leaders are required to grow in their positions :

And a Leader, to be successful, is expected to carry the following Traits -

TRAITS	DESCRIPTIONS
Drive	Desire for achievement; ambition; high energy; tenacity; initiative
Honesty and integrity	Trustworthy; reliable; open
Leadership motivation	Desire to exercise influence over others to reach shared goals
Self-confidence	Trust in own abilities
Cognitive ability	Intelligence; ability to integrate and interpret large amounts of information
Knowledge of the business	Knowledge of industry, relevant technical matters
Creativity	Originality
Flexibility	Ability to adapt to needs of followers

In a Retail Bank like scenario where a total team needs to work in tandem, the Leader needs to be part of the team as a member involving the team in every activity and bringing out the best of every individual member of the team. This generates motivation and skills are enhanced in people. The following Diagram will best explain my statement.

To add, a true Leader is like a father figure to his team members who can trust their leader, love him and appreciate his qualities. I feel like mention a person, Atul Barve, who was Regional Head in my team during my stay in IDBI Bank. Often I found him coming to me and to press for promotion or salary increase for many of his staff, especially during appraisal time. But never I had seen him speaking for himself. Atul is an example where a true leader elevation for his people more than for him. Here a leader stands apart.

To conclude this Leadership discussion:

- Establish relationship between Leadership Behavior & Decision Making
- Participation increases decision acceptance.
- Decision acceptance increases commitment and effectiveness of action.

Leadership Styles

In Banking industry, Leadership is mostly applicable in Retail Banking where involvement of manpower is huge and driving the work force is a challenge. During one's walk in the meadow of Retail Banking, one definitely comes across various types of leaders and variety of their leadership styles. In my long stint in Retail Banking, I have also met quite a number of personalities in the related business field. Let me recapitulate :

1. I met a Retail Banking guru. His knowledge in Retail Banking is not only unquestionable but is highly appreciated

across the industry. Always a smiling personality and easily approachable. He guides and gives advices to people and is highly methodical in his approach. However knowledgeable, he does not take advices from others. He listens to people, he smiles but does what he thinks right.

2. A young Retail Bank leader, Vikram Jetley had worked with me in three banks. Very young and brilliant, displayed Leadership of a different style. He was a team man in the true sense of the term. To him, team members are brothers and sisters. He works with them, guides them, mix with them like socially like a family member. He spend nights with the team and finally what I have seen, his force are diehard fans for him. He is a kind teacher, respected by all. Vikrams's leadership may be termed as Participative Leadership.

3. Mr. Gautam Vir who was known as a Turn Around Man in the industry is another example of Leadership. A proper blend of CITI and Standard Chartered culture, he empowers his people to generate profit for their respective vertical of business. At the same time he keeps his ears in the grass and drives every individual in his own concept of business. He creates a small trusted group of executives and exerts control over the situation. He listens to people, values their opinion and changes his style accordingly if needed. Gautam Vir is a leader of flexible nature. About rewarding people in the organization, I can't forget one advice from this cannon ball leader. He said " reward your performing employees before they ask for the same"

4. As opposed to the above three types of leaders, Mr. Ramanathan is a ruthless captain. A very sharp person in business understanding, he keeps his people under sticks and there is always a fear psychosis among his team members. A successful man in banking, he is unpopular among his team

members. Still, in the industry this type of leaders are seen and their style may be call Dictatorship.

5. I had an opportunity to work with another Retail Banker, Melvin Burger. A young and smart person driving a sizeable team as Head Retail, Melvin operates He is a leader with a mask. An ever smiling guy, Melvin mixes with his members in a very cordial way. The problem is, his people don't trust him as a person to confide. It results in a superficial relationship between leader and people.

6. The last example is Mr. Pilvit. He is a big contradiction between Trust and Disbelief. Due to his limited access to the depth of Retail Banking, he depends upon his team and goes all out to ensure progress for the performers. On the other hand, due to his Blue Blood pride he builds a team around him with a handful of people who also hail from rich families. The result is, the real performers get hurt and gradually detach themselves from the team. The second nature of Mr. Pilvit is, he is revengeful (as is commonly said). Hence people who divorce him, become cautious about his actions against them.

I am allured to draw reference to our epics to show two more styles of leadership. One is from Ramayana. *When Ramachandra decided to reach Lanka, the empire of Ravana, the army needed to cross the ocean for which a bridge was to be made. The Banar regiment of Sugreeva were engaged for this upheaval task and they had made no stone unturned to throw stones into the ocean and finally to build a bridge to Lanka. This was made possible for an unfailing loyalty and respect for their Supremo, Lord Rama.* Sometimes work forces are ready to do anything for their leaders.

Let us look at another style of leadership. *Before Mahabharata war Lord Krishna had told both Arjuna and Duryadhana that he would not take up arms during the war even though he might take one of the sides. During the whole war which had lasted for eighteen days, Sri Krishna had kept his word but all through the battle, he had played behind the screen, strategizing, planning, directing, motivating and often changing plans when necessary. The war was won by the Pandavas only due to the leadership of Krishna.* Was it not a unique example of Leadership?

What we get in nutshell as regards Leadership Styles :

- **Delegating**
    - o Low relationship/ low task
    - o Responsibility
    - o Willing employees
- **Participating**
    - o High relationship/ low task
    - o Facilitate decisions
    - o Able but unwilling
- **Selling**
    - o High task/high relationship
    - o Explain decisions
    - o Willing but unable
- **Telling**
    - o High Task/Low relationship
    - o Provide instruction
    - o Closely supervise

Employee Satisfaction

According to Srivastava & Rastogi (2008), the reason for turnover can be many but it can be finally zeroed down to one factor and that is, because the employee was dissatisfied with the organization.

Long ago one Retail Banking Guru remarked *"whether a bank performed well or bad in the past is evident from its balance sheet. If the bank is presently doing good or bad is known from the Customer Satisfaction survey. But how the same bank will fare in the future days can be known from its Staff Satisfaction survey. Only motivated staff, satisfied staff and skilled staff can drive an organization forward with desired success".*

Let us, then, take a short trip to the realm of Employee Satisfaction which is one of the very important areas as far as Retail Banking is concerned. Throughout the world across industry and organizations Employee Satisfaction is given serious importance. Organizations by themselves and various bodies often conduct Employees satisfaction survey. Even we find competition among organizations to declare "Best Company to Work". Now, why this is important? It is important because it is directly linked with the question of performance and eventually attrition of non-performers.

An employee who is not satisfied in his organization for whatever may be the reason, cannot perform. This lack of satisfaction may emerge from various factors as under :

> ➢ He does not like his nature of job hence cannot derive pleasure out of his daily work.
> ➢ His Superior may be an unfriendly person and does not bear any empathy for him.
> ➢ His Supervisor may be an unworthy person according to the employee and is not able to appreciate the good work done by the staff, hence frustration.
> ➢ His remuneration may not satisfy him and he thinks it is not related to market.
> ➢ His Performance Appraisal might have put him down.

All the above factors may contribute to the low delivery by an employee and he, in turn, feels himself down which lends to his performance.

EMPOWERMENT

Empowerment is a story that one cannot evade while talking about any industry whatsoever. In any Retail Bank, the success depends upon the extent and nature of empowerment that prevails there. While the whole vertical should move within the set policies and principles towards achievement, every employee, from at least

Manager level and upward needs to be empowered in his / her role to some extent. This has a far reaching effect as under :

1. Decision making power in an individual blooms and prepares him with confidence for higher responsibilities.
2. Sense of belongingness develops and sense of responsibility grows from within giving rise to commitment of the employee.
3. The Leadership quality comes out of the jobholder.
4. It gives birth to Delight in work place, hence delivery graph takes a north bound turn.

In this connection, it will be a slip if I don't mention the name of Mr. Gunit Chadha, former Managing Director, IDBI bank and Deutsche Bank in India. *Gunit in his inimitable style of functioning used to call his two down reporting line even in unexpected hours and used to check whether their immediate superiors were giving them adequate power to operate. Initially we used to respond in the way we should without understanding why he was so particular about empowerment. Later I realized how important Empowerment is in the interest of any organization.*

Meanwhile, we can take a quick glance at the various types of power that we come across ;

Basically there are two types of power being enjoyed by people and these are **(a) Positional Power and (b) Personal Power**. We find that Legitimate or *Positional power* arises out of an authority associated with a particular position in an organization. Next comes *Reward Power* which arises from the ability to grant rewards valued by others. We also face a negative power which is in other words *Coercive Power*. This is identified with people who use Power that emerges from the ability to punish behavior. Next comes *Expert Power* which is virtually a Power that is earned from knowledge or skill. *Expert should be credible, trustworthy and relevant.* Ending with *Personal power,* this is Power that arises from personality characteristics that command admiration, respect and identification.

In the industry we happen to meet, thus, various types of people who displays their power and exercise the same according to their position, characteristic trait, knowledge, skill and personality.

Powerless Employees :

In many of the banks we come across senior staff members who have grown with the bank giving blood for their organizations in the initial stage and have reached a point when, with change in Management they are only senior members. Banks, out of compassion, keep them in various positions as advisors, consultants e.t.c. While discussing this, a big Mahabharata character, Vishma, comes to mind. We may structure his appraisal and have a look. *Vishma the most revered character in the epic of Mahabharata was an unchallenged personality all through his life. Vishma was an embodiment of virtue, heroism, duties and so on. He never assumed the power of a king but was the guardian of the Kauravas and Pandavas ensuring that the kingdom is protected from enemies, that subjects stay happy and the empire to expand. His contribution was immense in the dynasty. But till death he didn't have any power, any say. He had to perform but witnessing the fall of the dynasty without anything for him to do. At the end he died a valiant death carrying respect of the world.* But if we construct an appraisal of this great soul, the following come out :

APPRAISAL OF GRANDFATHER VISHMA - HIS VOLUNTARY RETIREMENT

Grandfather Bhishma, the senior most member of Kuru dynasty, is on the bed of arrows awaiting the Sun to move to Uttarayan when he can volunteer his final retirement from his duties on earth. The initial wounds seem to have dried up and there is no oozing of blood now. But isn't his heart bleeding within ? His lips too want to come out of dryness but eyes are not. Tear drops come out to flow over his cheeks when he is alone under the star studded firmament with sounds of nocturnal creatures around intervals. Bhishma does his "Self Appraisal" for the first time at the end of his tenure.

WHAT WERE YOUR ACHIEVEMENTS ? Appraisee - Vishma

1. I sacrificed my family life to satisfy the voluptuous pleasure of his father.
2. I shouldered the duty of getting my step brother Bichitrabirja married and for that I forcefully abducted two princesses from Sayambhara. I had risked his reputation but delivered and created Amba, one of the girls, my enemy who caused my corporal downfall.
3. I brought up the Kaurava and Pandava princes including Dhritarastra and Pandu through process of Learning and Development.
4. As a regular and responsible courtier I guided Dhritarastra and his sons with good advices and directions.
5. Always I was watchful of developments and shared / discussed with senior officials and colleagues like Dronacharya, Kripacharya and Vidur.
6. Tried my best to act for "Damage control" by keeping Duryodhan and Junta away from war.
7. Finally I showed unconditional loyalty towards Kauravas and gave my last blood for the group.

COMMENTS OF THE APPRAISER :

- Pitamah Bhishma remained a responsible courtier all through his life and was loyal to the Kuru dynasty. He played the role of a formidable warrior of the kingdom and a noble adviser to the court.
- In very few cases his advices were taken seriously and followed while his physical energy and militia skill was exploited all through by the CEO and his close group.
- Starting from Dhritarastra to his sons, none could be developed into a matured and state personality in terms of virtues, rather they turned into a diabolic team.

- Bhishma's strong sense of ethics and morality came into clash with his uncompromising loyalty to the dynasty. Finally the latter won.
- Bhishma had enjoyed respect and reverence of all as a towering personality, though without assertiveness. But he never enjoyed power to determine course of action.

OBSERVATIONS By Janata :

a) An adviser's role is only an Honorary one unless he is empowered with decision making.

b) Organizations are often seen to have Advisory panel on the platform and their opinions, observations and advices are recorded in Minute books for transparency. But finally it is the CEO or some powerful Board members who take the call.

c) Whatever sacrifices can be made by an employee for the organization, if the Delivery is not positive and quantifiable, the Balanced Score Card shows low or negative numbers.

d) It is better to do periodic Self Appraisal sitting alone to understand one's current state of Equity in the organization

e) It's better for senior members of staff with high vintage to make one's way out before he is asked by the authorities – "When ?"

Here, I would like to mention the name of Mr. Gunit Chada, a renowned banking personality in India. As a Managing Director he was two levels above me both in IDBI Bank and Deutsche Bank. *During my attachment with him, I often found him asking me over phone or in person whether I was adequately empowered by my superior (Retail Head). Initially I wondered but later I realized that this is one of the great qualities of a true leader to ensure that employees at all levels enjoy freedom in decision making and feel the delight in work place.*

At the same time Empowerment should not boil down to trust in wrong person who may misuse or make faults in judgement in his own place and authority lands up in embarrassment.

EMPLOYEES IN MERGER & ACQUISITION SCENARIO

Ever since the new generation Private Sector banks entered the field during the last decade of the bygone century, we have been witnessing a line of merger and acquisition in the banking sector. The reasons are multiple starting from failure in running and strengthening a new bank, lack of management control, poor financial management and bad handing of asset portfolio. As a result we found a number of new generation banks like Centurion Bank, Global Trust Bank, Bank of Punjab and some more got swallowed by bigger and more successful banks in the industry. While in each case Government / RBI's decision was correct, the impact on employees was an issue which, though unavoidable, created stress on, especially the employees of the engulfed banks. Recently, PSU banks are also getting merged and there is no difference in the state of the employees. We have also seen the takeover of weak IDBI Bank by LIC. To have a clear idea about what may be the impact on employees due to such acquisition or merger, I am reproducing text of a short article as a thought over the takeover of IDBI Bank by LIC. The takeover is over and the amalgamation process is on. Let's have a look :

LIC MARRIES IDBI BANK

At the end of all speculations, assumptions, doubts and anxieties LIC have taken over IDBI Bank which has been limping for about a decade and was surviving with the periodical help from Govt of India. While much to observe in the coming days, let us look at the major challenge that the acquiring body will have to take up and solve adroitly. When there is any 'Take Over' in the industry, the key challenge that is faced is managing Human Resource. Balance sheet riddles, dispute of funding, reorganization of network e.t.c can be sorted out when brains meet over and over again with their sum total of experiences. But Human Resource is a long term headache that needs to be addressed with a clear understanding and satisfaction. One Retail Banking Guru once told me "Whether a bank has performed good, medium or bad in the past, is traceable from their balance sheet. Whether a bank is currently doing good, medium or bad is understood from their Customer satisfaction survey but to visualize whether a bank WILL perform good, medium or bad in future can, be discerned from their Staff satisfaction survey". Yes, only a team of motivated staff with knowledge, skills and experience can drive a bank to prosperity.

Although initially LIC needs to ensure cleaning the NPA in Advance (currently hovering around 30%) lying in IDBI Book by infusing huge amount of fresh fund, they cannot wait for long to start the ball of business rolling in a productive way on a clean slate thus wiping off the history of non-performance post reverse merger and exit of Mr. Gunit Chadha with his team. Let us look at the strengths and weaknesses of the state owned insurer.

Strengths :

1. Huge experience in Network management
2. Hands on with Customer services and grievance management
3. Experience in vast Field management on Indian soil.

Weaknesses :

1. No Banking experience
2. No Banking hands in the top brass to run profitably

If we look at the above five points, it becomes evident that the essentially Human Resource is what should come on the top three priorities. Why so ? Let us examine keeping an eye on reality :

a) The employees from top to bottom are already suffering from anxieties related to unforeseen redundancy leading to downsizing of work force, transfer to other locations, down grading, salary cut for cost cutting and so on.

b) This insecurity will gain strength probably after the forth coming annual general meeting which may be the last one of independent IDBI Bank.

I am receiving calls from my young brothers and sisters whom we left behind in IDBI Bank. I know, similarly brothers in senior management who were part of the team building IDBI Bank, are nurturing tensions. For all of them my errand is as below :

a) Had your bank been engulfed by another stalwart bank, there would have been enough space for anxieties on various fronts. But it is not so. LIC will have to run the sick bank with Profit, and profit only. They don't have People in the related field. Hence, they need all performing guys in the middle and lower racks.

b) As regards Executives high up in the ladder, LIC cannot trust all individuals. They may go for a marrow change to replace a considerable number of heads since the Top management could not run the bank in the way a bank should be. But even saying so, they cannot ignore experienced and vibrant senior hands who were part of original IDBI Bank. I am sure that body language and personality of such handful people, who I know, will help the new management identify this efficient group.

c) For management of the huge network of branches, LIC will have to depend on the present workforce and they will be wise to do so. These are the people who are still maintaining the excellent quality of customer service at par with new generation private sector banks. But "shape up or ship out" message should be kept in mind by these groups since infusion of new blood cannot be eliminated.

However, employees across ranks will have to be prepared for the following to come :

1) Down grading of people, for example CGM to GM or GM to DGM and on.
2) Restructuring the compensation module
3) Reformation of Organization structure
4) Reorganization of Branch network

All the above are expected in view of a massive reduction in cost of operation and since in any organization Employee cost occupies the major portion of the pie, it's the employees who may be suffering most but on the brighter side, there won't be any big brother to trample them on the mat as it happens often when a stronger bank takes over a weaker one.

For LIC, it will be a big mistake if they meditate to bring in mid-career talents from competition in a mass It will turn into inflow of non-performing hands who are on the exit list or are just keeping afloat in their current organization. Moreover, LIC won't be able to offer attractive compensations to allure real talents hence those who are in weak wickets in other banks may make foray with compromise.

It's a fact that top management should be reorganized. In such cases, people with excellent track record and drive in private sector or foreign banks should come on board to bring back the bank to its original glamour during early part of the last decade.

It's not that the scenario will be same in each case of acquisition or merger. It varies from case to case. For example, if it is a merger of two PSU banks, the risk of losing job is less but possibility of transfer to remote places is high. In case the affair is between two private sector banks, there is much to worry since in top level there won't be much scope to accommodate all in senior positions. Again cost cutting may affect the employees of acquired entity. Given the present scenario in the world of merger and acquisition and its effect on the employees and also the typical HR related challenges being faced by Management, what can be the solution ? I think, the solution is hidden in Conflict and Change Management. Let us spend some lines on this.

The recent mega decision of the Finance Ministry to merge a number of PSU banks thus reducing the number of PSU banks to 10 will become a big challenge for the Human Resource verticals to mix people of various cultural back ground and geography into common platforms. There will be a number of changes like merger of multiple branches of the amalgamated banks in one location. This will surely bring down the cost but the problem that will surface is to utilize surplus manpower where there is little chance of people losing job. In such scenario, VRS will be an automatic outcome while career progression of the surviving employees will be at jeopardy. It will also take a long time to blend employees of different bank into a harmony. An immediate pandemonium is envisaged where there will be conflicts at all corners for HR to handle. At top management level number of positions will be drastically reduced where people will have to resort to VRS since there will be very little opportunity for the PSU people to get berth in Private Sector banks, not to talk of Foreign Banks where there will be a big cultural mismatch for the insured group hunting for places.

CONFLICT & CHANGE MANAGEMENT :

In literature it is said, "No conflict, no Drama". Like in life, our work place is also a dramatic platform where there are conflicts among characters, in interest, expression, style of working and, of course, Expectations. Retail Banks essentially deal with big number hands and it is always a challenge to manage these conflicts on an ongoing basis. It is up to the HR vertical to be vigilant on these conflicts and be proactive to identify the problem areas, causes and to ensure that these are eliminated before the eruption.

Conflicts, it is generally seen, are of two types – Organizational and Interpersonal.

Manage interpersonal conflict

Office related politics, personality mismatch and such other causes give birth to clashes between individuals who join the organization from various walks of life, with diverse experience carrying different types of work culture. These need to be nipped in the bud for the best interest of the bank.

A Retail Bank moves with certain mission and vision which are common in the particular organization. Hence, Interpersonal conflicts will only damage the movement and unless there is a perfect team work.

HR needs to encourage people to work in tandem focusing on goals rather than brooding over trivial matters. If specific interpersonal problem is identified, HR is expected to intervene and stop the ball rolling further to deterioration. Often we find one or two de-motivator in the team. These de-motivators are to be identified and separate from the team.

How to defuse organizational conflict

Organizational conflict is most often identified in hierarchy related issues. Conflict in interests and dissatisfaction over expectations are root causes in workplaces. It has its origin in various points like resource allocation, work pressures, accountability or any situation where discrimination are marked in groups of people. It's of paramount importance to address these issues. Suggested routes are:

1. Ignore trivial issues but keep watch on development.
2. HR may act as mediator involving head of the related business vertical or any other responsible official.
3. To find out a common platform where the conflicting parties express satisfaction. A win-win situation, after compromising by both the sides, is to be created.

When none of the above techniques works, a forced decision by competent authority may be the solution to end the tussle.

Change to Defuse Conflict

Change is a reality in life. In a bank, it can be caused by growth, pursuing new ventures, management turnover or policy changes. Most people are unsettled by change, however, which gives rise to conflict. A good change management is essential to drive and defuse conflict. Change needed due to change in market situation, geographical shift, merger and acquisition and cost control. Although human being are basically averse to Change, there is no alternative but to accept Change and to cope up with it.

On the other hand, Management must be prepared and positioned to see ensure that Change is handled adroitly. Open communication is also necessary to maintain transparency. Employees should be informed and kept updated on circumstances causing changes and what is being considered in response. By being transparent and keeping them in the loop, they'll be less resistant and conflicted by change.

CONCLUSION

Thus ends the story of Retail Banking in India. It is the story of expectations of people at different segments and at different levels of financial standing. It is the story of how this new vertical of banking emerged out of the need of people and how bankers as teams are dedicated towards making it happen in the best possible way making the business meaningful for their organizations. Retail Bank is truly "of the people, for the people and by the people." It is the story of developing Life Styles of billions of people in India where IT revolution also has its big role as a support zone, where Human Resource management is a mighty pillar to roll the ball.

The story of Retail Banking will continue with the growth of economy and with the change in Lifestyle of Janata across the plane. Life moves, society marches forward and with it the likes and dislikes also take shapes in human mind. Retail Banking is a depiction of the behavioural pattern of the individuals of the contemporary age and the very nature of this vertical will change from time to time with the socio economic changes in India. We look forward to the tales of the future. It will be written by authors of the coming days when today's story will take place in the annuls of history - The History of Retail Banking.

About the Authors

Gautam Gan, an eminent Retail banking personality in India, has travelled through ten banks, both Foreign and Private sector, picking up bits of experiences with related skills and success. This long banking experience of 35 years was added to his association with Micro-finance world for another 3 years touching the bottom most line of population and their world. During his journey through the financial sector the writer, with his keen interest in human psychology and humanity, nurtured Retail banking in the depth of his heart and blended his own life with this area of human science. The outcome was his first book "The Confessions of a Banker" published in 2016 with a ripple in the related market. An MA in English literature, Gautam Gan known to his huge friends and relatives as a poet too who already published "Ratnabali" and Nourelle" two books of poetic composition. The present book "Retail – The Lifestyle Banking" is the author's sincere effort to present Retail Banking in a completely different perspective far beyond the general notion of this business vertical which is essentially based on human psychology, human expectation, dream and also frustration.

Sreyashi Gan is the co-author of "Confessions of a Banker". Daughter of Gautam Gan, this young lady is a Human Resource professional with a background in Psychology. On completion of her MSc in International Human Resource Management from United Kingdom, she is now working in the area of Learning and Development with Dale Carnegie. Her poem "Looking Back" was published by Greenspring Publishing, USA, in their collection of poetic works "Voices" where among 56 poets her composition was the only poem representing Asia. A strong passion for literature and psychology, Sreyashi has actively shouldered her contribution to the Human Resource part of the book

Udayan Gan Chowdhury is the Gautam Gan's son and has penned the IT aspect of this book. Udayan is an IT professional with academic background (MBA) in Finance and specialization in Banking. Currently a Senior Manager with Accenture Australia, Udayan has more than 10 years of experience implementing IT systems and consulting for the major banks in Australia across different banking domains playing the roles of Business Analyst, Business Architect, Project Manager and Program Manager. Udayan is recognized for his bringing thought leadership and innovation through business process re-engineering to global banking firms to improve their operations and customer experience.

Memories